Bimini Twists

Bimini Twists
A Short Fiction

SANDY RODGERS

THE DERRYDALE PRESS

Lanham and New York

THE DERRYDALE PRESS

Published in the United States of America by
The Derrydale Press
4720 Boston Way, Lanham, Maryland 20706

Distributed by NATIONAL BOOK NETWORK, INC.

This is a work of fiction.
Any resemblence to persons living or dead is coincidental.

Library of Congress Cataloging-in-Publication Data

Rodgers, Sandy (Sandy Gean)
    Bimini twists : a short fiction / Sandy Rodgers.
       p. cm.
    ISBN 1-58667-055-7 (cloth : alk. paper)
    I. Title.

    PS3568.O45565 B56 2001
    813'.6—dc21
                                                            00-046583

⊗™ The paper used in this publication meets the minimum requirements of
American National Standard for Information Sciences—Permanence of
Paper for Printed Library Materials, ANSI/NISO Z39.48-1992.
Manufactured in the United States of America.

To Bob, for everything.

Contents

ONE

The Last Good Day of Fishing Was the Day before You Came

Skip jerked awake. He squinted his filmy eyes at the ticking alarm and flinched in readiness for its irritation. He focused. Another half dial remained. So why did he wake up—God's truth, he could use about three days of extra rest. Then the sour burst of remembrance pumped bile—he faced another day tarpon fishing with two clients spawned in hell. Who could sleep with that kind of boil leaking its infective horrors into your dream stream?

He twisted and peered at his sleeping wife Shelly, a small mountain range rising tangled from short vanilla hair and sloping past cradle hips. Her face wore crescent smudges below the shuttered lids. Getting to both of them, this pace, though it would severely piss her off if he told her so.

He unfolded, stiff, from the edge of the bed. He asked himself whose great idea lightbulb flash to blame anyway, the idea to run a boat, take people fishing. A guide. It must have sounded like "god" in his head when he thought it all up. Yeah, out on the sparkling blue flats of the Florida Keys sucking in the balmy salt air and the glory of getting paid for finding fish. Living the immediate life of full-on reality, not the vicarious, unscented, colorless TV shadow of a life so common anymore, yeah. Now he knew that if people measured jobs for degree of difficulty like some Olympic high dive or gymnast leap, fishing guide would rank high in terms of endless hours and aching muscles. Glory? No such thing as glory out there hemorrhaging sweat and getting epoxy-headed flies slammed into what's left of the meat on his sun-dried scaly limbs while the varicose veins crawled up his legs, snapping like rubber bands in a sixth-grade classroom. But he hadn't broken many bones. Glamorous job.

Skip steered down the Overseas Highway toward the boat ramp, chewing on a couple coffee grounds that had strayed into his back teeth. The hot sweet wind, scented with frangipani and lycaloma, did little to cool his window arm. Or any of him. He wished he had fixed the air conditioning in this old truck before it turned so hot; now it was too late to matter. But the radio worked. It spewed out a driving pulse of vintage rock, road music to wake him up, which faded into a buzz of ear pain as he passed local radio transmitters. He ground his molars, tapped his fingers, considered how time compressed and expanded.

He pictured Shelly curled back around the bed pillows, time for her slowed on the surface but fast inside, days turned into hours, whirling in her fantastic dreams of Day-Glo creatures from a surreal menagerie. Then she'd wake with the perception mere minutes had passed. Meanwhile, tires humming, he barreled down the siren-filled, neon-uglied, lane-changing assholes road, everything fast outside but taking lots of head time. Good thing they had clocks, sunshine, darkness. If you went by how it felt everyone would live in unmatched realities.

Skip loaded the two paragons of fly fisherdom into his skiff at duck hunting o'clock, delighted to see that one of them had actually strung his rod and tied on a fly. Learned something from yesterday—make an angler out of this one yet, yeah. His peg moved up to rookie. His companion started right off puling about his terminal hangover, like it came as a big surprise he had to get up early this morning. He'll think terminal if he chunks on my boat. Hangover had been a referral from another guide who claimed he had overbooked. Overbooked my ass, he just didn't want to listen to this crap for another year. Couldn't blame him, though. Maybe the rookie with the live functioning brain would make the day for them. Hope so. Turn him into a regular.

They skimmed over the mercury smooth water through the dawn, narrowly outrunning two other guides redlining their outboards for the same choice spot. Tough luck, butt plugs. They might beat him tomorrow but today counted. He might even call them tonight and laugh about it, but this time of year the race went to the swift and the brutal. The hellish season had unfurled.

Skip poled into the last whisper of liquid night and watched the streaks of morning brighten his world. Roseate spoonbills on their way to work reflected an omen of pink hope. Then he spotted a pod of barely awake tarpon. They floated toward the skiff breathing softly of the watered air, fins out, eyes dreamy, and he rasped a stage-whispered alert to his clients: "Look! Fifty yards! See their backs out of the water!" God these fish only needed to see a fly in front of them, a shrimp or fish or crab-looking fly, and one'd suction it into its heavy metal jaw and explode into the morning with the primal dance that made anglers' hearts stand still, that made guides keep doing it.

But Hangover still sat piddling around with his leader and fly. Because for chrissake why should he bother to string up the goddamn rod before he got on the boat like Skip asked him to yesterday. Because these thoughtful, yes, sensitivity-trained New Age tarpon would, of course, wait for the proper karmic moment to swim by Hangover's Cockroach. Because where he hailed from he downsized companies and ruined lives, and was accustomed to having things done on His Time. Because his memory was as short as his dick.

Rookie stepped up to the casting platform, looked back at Skip, tentative.

"Go for it!" Skip urged him. "Lay it down nice and easy."

Rookie peeled out line, waved it, aimed, fired. And whapped the fly into the side of the skiff. Skip winced, but splattercasters were as numerous as mosquitoes in Flamingo. Something about a nicely tied fly just made people ache to beat their painted beady eyes against the boat. Rookie turned, dismay melting his face. They all frowned as the school of giant fish glided away, armor shining.

"At least you gave it a try." Skip grinned at him, then swung down from the tower to re-sharpen the hook or get out another fly. "But there went your lifetime quota of perfect shots," he teased. But it was the truth.

Another thing that brightened his life like gum on his flip-flops was how some dudes picked up a high-recognition outfit at a fly shop and thought for sure 'cause it cost a stack of Franklins it made them experts. Hoping the mystique of the brand would inject them with skill, rub off onto their untrained arms like unresined fiberglass. Excalibur the Rod. Never mind learning how to cast the bigger rod, heavier line, maybe into some wind, before they got here, no sir. They'll just clamber onto the boat and somehow magically, because the guide stands back there on The Tower and possesses godlike powers and can make everything fishy happen with a stroke of his pushpole, magically they'll manage to shoot seventy feet of fly line into a fifteen knot wind. Yeah.

"I'm nowhere near you!"

By noon Skip knew he believed in miracles, because it was truly a miracle he hadn't turned into a mass murderer, gone berserk and used his pushpole as a jousting lance or maybe a javelin and run through these bozos who refuse to give anyone enough space on a flat to fish! "You just cut in front of me not thirty feet from my boat and you call that nowhere near?" His voice rose spiraling to the brink, cracking free of control. Major pissed.

"Hey man, you don't own the water."

The stock answer. Why did they bother? He'd heard it so many times he could say it for them. They could kick back in the hot tubs of their goddamn Miami ice cream condos, spread some bacteria around, and not even come down here with their bimbos in circus garb and get in everyone's way and he could just fax them, let them know he whined: "Hey man, you don't own the water," for them five or six times that day.

But these guys were civilians, not guides; obvious they Don't Know Any Better. He tried another tack. A deep breath. "Okay guys, I guess you don't understand. What we're doing here is fishing along this flat on a migratory path of the tarpon and we cast to them as they come by. When you come screaming across that path with your boat you scare whatever fish were heading this way, and my clients here don't get a shot at them. So whenever you see a boat like this with a guy standing on the tower poling or looking for fish, the thing to do is give him as much room as possible. And please don't cut right in front, try to go behind, okay?"

Hangover and Rookie, on whose behalf Skip had made this long for him speech, stood behind him, cowed somewhat by the confrontation but at least not cringing like little gut worms on the seat. Maybe they realized that he was fighting for their opportunity to catch these fish they had traveled so far and paid so much to lob flies at.

The dickhead guys and 'bos looked amazed that any of this held such importance. "Wow, man, we didn't mean to mess you up, but this is our swimming hole, man."

Resignation clenched Skip's heart as he watched their phallic drug courier boat drift away a few feet on the wind. They tossed out an anchor and splashed their sundry bodies into the tourmaline water behind it for their refreshing swim. Right into the only good white sand hole to spot tarpon over for a mile. Time to look for fish somewhere else. Maybe China.

The sad part—some of the guides acted almost as bad, pretending ignorance of the local protocols. Like day before yesterday.

Skip had met his angler at oh-dark-thirty and enriched an oil company to the section of Tarpon Trail he wanted to fish first. Though they needed to wait for a higher sun angle to see incoming fish well—unless they rolled or finned out—the necessity of staking a claim demanded it. Like duck hunting. The skiff swooshed off plane, Skip poled in shallower. Not another boat in sight. Good.

Three blown shots at bubbleheads later another guide boat streaked up on the outside and shut down, parallel. Skip knew him, saw him pretend not to notice as his skiff drifted with the wind, edging in front. Old Two and Two Skip had nicknamed him. As in the difference between hiring him as a guide or renting a boat and fishing on your own? Two hundred pounds and two hundred dollars.

Skip stood with his hands on his hips. Obvious the butthead was ignoring him, in fear of the inevitable. "Hey! What do you think you're doing?" he yelled, fulfilling expectations.

Two's head whipped around in a pretense of surprise. Skip threw up his arms in a gesture of disbelief, then stroked toward him hard, murder in his heart. This guy knew better, he fumed, he's just trying to burn me. No way. I'll board his boat, I'll . . . he didn't know what. One guide he knew kept a baseball bat on his skiff, but Skip figured a pushpole would suffice.

The intimidation worked.

Two had cranked up—instead of poling to avoid disturbing the fish, of course—and put-putted away, still pretending: all a big mistake, no offense or anything, but I'll just cut in on you 'cause I was too lazy to haul my worthless ass out of bed early enough to claim the spot, and I saw you hook one here the other day so I know it's good, and even though I never fished here before in my wannabe life, now it'll be that spot We like to fish whenever I call you on the phone.

Skip had hawked and spit, thinking, Like we're still old buddies after he slimes me like that. Like we ever were.

Back in the sun dog blinding afternoon with Rookie and Hangover, Skip grunted and huffed and sweated his soul near heatstroke to get around a dozing tarpon. She lay in the warm surface water, content, going nowhere, a flawless inclusion in the emerald liquid. Skip humped the boat into perfect position after fifty miles and three days of dehydration, and Hangover started flailing away.

Six casts later he hadn't come close but the enormous fish began to sense all the attention paid to her piece of ocean. She stirred, burped a bubble of air, fluttered a pectoral. The seventh cast piled down leaving the leader at the bottom of a puddle of citron flyline. "Pick it up, easy!" Skip shouted in a whisper. When Hangover mulishly decided to strip it anyway the fly headed in a direct line of attack toward the drowsy tarpon. Information anomaly. Knowing well that nothing she might choose to eat would zip toward her in such a merry and reckless manner, she assumed the need for an emergency response. She squirted away like a grape—a memory vision of boil of foam and streak of blue. Skip sighed. Tears of sweat bled down his cheeks. Might as well have a shark on the boat.

Twelve hours past morning he backed his skiff between the palm trees and the sea grapes. He unloaded rods and embraced the indoors, his parched body ready to sponge up the cold, quench the core fire that sunburned from within, Amazing how he'd drink gallons of water and not have enough moisture left to wring out a decent pee. A cold beer later he returned to the rippling heat and washed the boat, cleaned the cooler, found the front hatch clip vibrated loose and the bow light burned out. Fixed them. Took the gear in, washed it, checked the leaders for wind knots. Fixed them.

Sometimes, Skip groused to Shelly that evening, he could eat a gun but it seemed too merciful. Something in a derringer, sir? Perhaps stainless? Hell, yes, wouldn't want to make a mess. No, might as well keep suffering—he was getting used to it, getting good to him. Next thing he'd begin sneaking orders from some brown paper wrapped S&M bondage catalog, hoping for a good flog. Be like a day on the boat lately.

Yeah, what a swell tarpon season. It had even started off weird, with a long cold spring and winds so stiff that the flags on the pandemic dive shops flapped in tight horizontals. Then it had belched without pardon right into the steamroom of summer. Dragging with it the frayed tempers of too many guides bummed by the frustrated efforts of rabid tarpon fishers. Skip already looked forward to the relative peace of stroking after bonefish and yelling at jet skis.

The phone rang. A new client wanted to chat about what kind of flies to tie, what kind of gear Skip had, as if he used rinky-dink cartoon outfits from the local dime-store. Then again, a few of the sleazeballs at the alcohol-soaked marina guide mills used shit for tackle, so maybe the guy had a point. Maybe he'd been stuck on one of their sewer barges once, wanted a quality experience for his dollar instead. Then he wanted to know what the weather would do by the time he arrived. Skip laughed, said if he could answer that last one why would he push a boat around for a living. Shit, he could just call in, tell everyone what the weather had planned and kick back and collect major bucks for his psychic skills. Yeah, one nine hundred psychic weather guide hotline.

He sighed into the shower. The phone rang again, this time another guide. He wanted to know how Skip did where he fished today, wanted to lie about how many tarpon he jumped, gloat a little, especially if Skip's day had blown buttloads, it seemed. After dinner the phone rang again and a good buddy wanted a fishing report, hint, hint, and hey, it sure would be swell to go after tarpon with him sometime soon. Yeah. Buddy. Invited himself and never paid for the boat ramp or the gas. What if Skip showed up where he worked and begged for whatever he did or made or sold for free, say a free three hundred dollar root canal. Which is how it felt anymore when this guy called. Skip put him off graciously, telling the truth: he didn't have any days off coming up.

Finally, uninterrupted couch time. Shelly turned on the answering machine and popped a movie into the VCR

while he settled back to watch. For about fifteen minutes, until his eyelids crashed to his cheeks. All over, time to fall out and start again from the bottom of the hill. Did he really choose this life or get condemned to it?

The next morning rumbled with thundering in the dark pearl sky as Skip helped his leggy client's small wife into the skiff. These were good people. Anglers. If the fish cooperated—some days they swam happy and ate like fourteen-year-old boys, some days they partied with Neptune—and if Tall and Tiny remembered what they learned last year, it could happen. Man, he felt long overdue. Seemed like everything that could screw up lately, had.

He tuned a wary ear to the vibrations of his outboard as they skimmed across the brine silk of the water. And thought how his brand new winch had started to sound like a cement mixer grinding rocks yesterday. He shut down, watched an osprey plunge toward breakfast—*he* was catching fish. Well, the winch would just have to chew the ore a while, 'cause he didn't have time, fast, slow, or any other kind, to mess with it.

Blush light painted the rippled bay while he poled, murmured for his people to get ready. They unracked their strung rods, exclaimed at a turtle with its bronze dishpan shell and alien eyes, took a couple turns casting, loosened up.

Then a fin like a black scimitar slid toward them, defining a dark back, a wagging tail. Oh god, a permit. Here they stood all set for tarpon and one of the impossible almost sacred fish to fly rodders pops up to stutter their hearts. "Sixty feet, point your rod! Yes! Cast! Cast!" Tiny jumped to attention, false cast a couple times, and flung her tarpon fly toward the unnamed shape. "More right! Pick it up, try again, hurry!" Skip didn't tell her she'd cast to a permit. Probably make her miss the shot. Permit were so unpredictable and hard to catch, why not try a tarpon fly on one. A bonefish fly. Season tickets. She hail Mary'd one out there. "Good. Perfect. Wait, strip it, strip it, slower, easy, wait. Okay, okay, he's got it, set up on him, set up!"

The line hummed, taut, and a supernova moon flash lit the water as the brilliant disc turned and ran. Tiny squeaked in excitement, her reel zinged and line smoked out the rod guides. Skip hollered, "Perm!" and honked after it, elated. He reveled in the rainbow wash of sky, the salt muck, the sandalwood incense from mangroves on a nearby key. This lucky blessing heaven fish.

Tiny's elbows trembled as bad as her knees but she maintained, pumping and reeling and giggling. Skip staked and hopped off the tower to help her land the gleaming icon, take pictures. She gasped when she held her first permit, at its large dark eyes that rolled up at her, soft wet and smart, its pouty lower lip, and butter-toned belly.

"Oh god," she said, "it feels like skin, like the inside of satin, not scales! It's gorgeous! How could anyone kill such a perfect thing?"

Skip snapped shots of their dazzled faces with the permit and murmured his agreement. He gently eased it into the olivine water, pushing to give its gills a big rush of oxygen, waiting for a kick of its jet tail signaling its readiness for a safe release. An angler needed to take special care of a charitable permit like this one, one that eats flies, by god. Damn if he could figure out why some people greased them. Far as he was concerned they swam right on top of his flats fish totem—permit, tarpon, bonefish—and it amounted to sacrilege, period.

He always marveled at how they would sneak up on him, like playing games with a mirage. Him poling, crunch grunt drip, up a glossy flat looking for boneys and then feeling that feather duster tickle on the back of his neck and looking around behind him and, yeah. A permit or several cruising in his blind spot like holograms, an illusion of fishiness until they turned up their rheostats for an instant and showed themselves, ebony fins and mirrors. He could almost imagine them snickering when he'd call attention to his anglers: "This'll get their hearts going, tee hee hee, make sure they see us, okay now disappear, tee hee." Going to give somebody a coronary. Aerobic cardiac stress test fish.

Skip poled back to the Tarpon Trail. Next came the hard part—hours that felt like years, strung long with anticipation, waiting for the fish to move while he amused his anglers with socially unacceptable jokes. Then the breathless excitement when he spotted a wad of tarpon, keeping his people from losing it, their knees gone to quivering. But who wouldn't tremble, sensing the strength of those huge torpedoes aiming for them? Hell, his knees shook, too, didn't matter how many times he saw their prehistoric majesties.

Today had started good, his only lingering worry those massing thunderheads. He'd nearly been smacked by lightning last summer. He had watched boomers pile up over the Everglades, still far enough away, when a bolt out of the blue struck right behind the skiff. His graphite pushpole had hummed like a swarm of killer bees as he flung himself onto the deck, yelling at his angler "Put down your rod! Get down!" then flash! boom! his hands numb to his shoulders for the rest of the day. Made a believer out of him. Now when those jagged shards of electricity started ripping through the air, he hauled ass.

But now a dark cloud of tarpon loomed. Tall made ready and they all made silly remarks, goofing, trying to ease the choke of tension, waiting for the fish to come in range of his cast. It happened. Like time-lapse film: the huge mouth of the tarpon opening into a bottomless white pit, slurping in the fly, turning away unconcerned, going back to important tarpon business, and Tall yanging on the line hard, hard, hard. And the tarpon, insulted, hurtling out of the shattered water like a pillar of belief in all goodness, virtue, and perfection, rattling metallic gill plates, silver an understatement, chrome, heart stopper stand up fish, outraged dancing on the foam, then crashing back splash and taking the short fast route to the Gulf of Mexico.

"All right!" Skip pursued the greyhounding tarpon for forty minutes that gasped like seconds to him. But weeks to Tall, whose office muscles cramped and groaned and begged for relief but who was so goddam happy he'd stand there and fight this fish until his arms fell goddam off if that's what it took. He pumped and laughed and bowed and reeled the tarpon close enough to the boat for Skip to leader her and get pictures of her cobalt-jeweled beauty. Unhooked and revived her. All right, Skip thought again. Maybe he'd stick with this business after all.

When later Tiny duplicated her husband's feat with another drink blender tarpon dance, Skip knew for sure that he'd broken his snake bit streak. Man, wait until he told Shelly tonight—good news for a change instead of tales of how his guys fucked off fish or didn't set up on them or forgot to bow and they came unhooked. Sure, even if you did everything right a tarpon could come unbuttoned. Just made it easier for success when the angler did his part. Yeah. He poled back to the right depth and got lined up again, asked Tiny if maybe she wanted to look for some bonefish, they had about an hour left, get the third part of her Grand Slam. Sometimes bones rooted around on this bank snuffling like little pigs, young brat brothers wanting to hang out with the big guys. Sometimes not. Other places held better odds. She and Tall mulled this over—leave hungry tarpon for bonefish? Meanwhile Skip made a routine check of the horizon.

"Holy shit!" he blurted. "We've got a water spout! Look!"

Their eyes followed his point and blew up like balloons at the bruised cotton cloud with the wispy, sooty fingers waving down from it. Tentacles of evil intent, one had formed into a steel wool cylinder that reached to the water. Sucking it up, spinning it to eternity, a fascinating doom pipe drumming toward them. No question now. They'd run for cover. If they couldn't make it to the boat ramp they could duck under one of the giant concrete bridges that carried the Overseas Highway across the channels between Keys. This kind of thrill would wow Tiny and Tall's friends back at the office, friends who felt all wiggly with risk when they left the skin on their broiled chicken. Yeah, narrowly missing being vacuumed up and spit out in shreds somewhere like Kansas, or worse, a section of downtown Miami, where if you survived the watery tornado someone would take care of that problem by running over you with their car after they looted your battered body. What a day.

Skip backed his boat into the driveway, heady from tarpon musk, anxious to share his happiness. Old Two and Two'd shit green for a week when he heard. A great day on the water. Everything he could hope for, well, maybe if Tiny had nailed her Grand Slam it could have been better, put him in line for some product endorsements like a real fish god or something. Or not. But it all measured up to the reasons he loved it. Yeah.

The house sat full of thick quiet and cool conditioned air. He nudged the setting lower, heard the motor kick in, joining its electric drone with the rest of the giant cicadas in the neighborhood. Thought she'd be home by now, usually was. Huh. He glanced at the answering machine, blinking, ignored it and went to the fridge and popped a cold one. Sat on a stool at the kitchen counter, stared at his salted, dried up, crusty, beat up feet, took a swig, stared at the line cuts on his hands, the can beading in them. Where could she be? A big dry hole yawned under his breastbone.

A guide he knew, his old lady had up and split on him, no wonder really since he called her that, but anyway, just grabbed her purse and the rat holed money he had stashed and farewell MF'd him. No, not Shelly, man, she wouldn't do that, she'd say something if she got bummed at him, at their life. Wouldn't she? But how well did he understand her strange woman mind? He thought of how all tarpon season he'd talked on the phone with his guide buddies until she glared, warning tracers shooting from amber eyes that dinner would not wait another minute, dammit. Then the phone might ring during dinner and another guide might want to shoot the shit so he ate and talked at the same time. Shelly'd sigh and cut his roast beef so he could eat with one hand. So where was she? Man, he wouldn't make her wait dinner anymore, he swore. What if today's perfection had only set him up for a big blindside rug puller of a shock? He wanted to look in the closet, see if her clothes still hung there, but he was too tired, yeah, too tired. Shitfire. Cobwebs formed. He took another swig of hop water and felt his hair turning gray. Now what?

Outside, the pearock crunched under the roll of tires. Then the thump of tennis shoes hurried up the steps to beat the mosquitoes and Shelly bounced through the door. He stood up and wrapped his arms around her, all salty and relieved, crushing her to the starched sweat of his tee shirt.

The phone rang.

TWO

 *Scent Trail*

An endless snag in a year of distress. That's how Skip and Shelly came to think of it, since the day they went salmon fishing with her dad, Ben.

Snapping photos, Shelly had soaked up the essence of the coastal rain forest like a sponge for majesty. The three of them skirted the mossy bank of a dream-perfect river, the winding path softened quiet as a cathedral by damp russet leaves and pine needles. Random clumps of rusty boletus and golden chanterelles flanked the way. The tangy air flushed her cheeks and pinched her nostrils with its chill. Fall at this latitude smelled to her like the snapping juice of a crisp apple.

Shelly paused on a fallen cedar and tissued off her lens, while Skip eased over smooth gray rocks to the lip of an emerald pool. He sought migrating salmon holding in the deep, at rest before their next run upstream through swift currents and rapids. Ben waited nearby in the shadow of pines, his racking cough muffled by a faded blue bandanna.

He had always coughed, especially in the morning. Sinus, he'd say. He shuddered with the last spasm, turned to spit furtively onto the humus. Hurried to nudge wet leaves over the spot with his boot, but not soon enough to hide the telltale streak of red.

Shelly's voice came out tight, "You should see a doctor."

He grunted, "Hell, Squirt, they can't help."

She bit her lip at his lifelong distrust of all things medical, while dread ripped her heart.

Ben hooked and landed a Chinook salmon that day that must have weighed forty-five pounds. Easy. Scales like slivers of ocean, with barely a tinge of the sunset colors that would bloom on its cheeks and sides, soon, at spawning. Skip had soared, honored to guide Ben through the struggle, though he noticed that while Shelly clicked pictures of them with the magnificent fish, Ben's arms and legs shook. With pride, sure—a fly rod-caught salmon warranted a healthy measure of that—but Skip feared the hypothermic tremble implied grave weakness. As if Ben's core had gone cold.

They released the fish to fulfill its purpose. It would continue upriver, guided by the unique scent of its home stream, dig a redd in the fine bottom gravel with its tail, lay its eggs, then station itself to guard the nest against predation until its end came. Its nutrient-rich body would help sustain the tiny lives it created as it returned itself completely to the stream where it first swam.

"Brutal, elegant continuum of life," Shelly whispered, face veiled in sad acceptance. She watched the salmon thrust itself away. With a powerful kick of its tail it swam resolutely toward its appointment with fate.

Since that day the year had clocked around, with winter steelhead, spring shad, summer runs. And then this morning:

"Oh!" Shelly's reflection turned pasty. She twisted away from her mirror image.

"Shelly? What's wrong?" Skip pried at her silence.

Her clammy forehead crimped into a frown. "I thought, no, I know I smelled that, um, scent—like when Freckles. . . ."

"That was ages ago." Painful memory. He leaned against the dresser.

She twiddled her hairbrush. "It smelled so—real."

He knew what was twisting her up, offered, "How about I call your Mom? Just to check."

Shelly paced the bedroom, unstrung, agitated. Back to the mirror. "Dark circles, no color. Great look for work." She dabbed on rosy blusher but it didn't hide the tightness underneath, or the worry pooling in her eyes. "We just saw him yesterday, and, I mean, he didn't. . . ."

Her father lay stretched on the hospital bed, stoic and emaciated. His face evoked a wax carving, all sharps and hollows, while his eyes had burned with the sight of a distant goal. She had pressed her cheek against his, felt the scrape of his white stubble. He smelled of soap and clean sheets. "We'll be back Wednesday, I love you," she whispered.

Skip nodded, watchful, serious. "Hon, he can't last."

She clenched her jaw to keep her mouth firm. For a year she had raged at the evil thing stealing her father, sucking away his last months into a blur of pain. The unfairness of it tied her stomach in knots, and she burned to fight the evil, squash it like a bug. But nothing could. Not even her hardheaded old dad.

She gasped in a desperate lungful, pressed her temples, swallowed hard. "No need to call. I'm just sleepy, that's all." She frequently jerked awake, thinking she heard the phone. Even asleep her mind listened for The Call, maintained its unconscious cringe from the imminent. Which loomed as certain as tears at a wedding. "Better get my act together, I'll be late."

Skip pulled her gently by the wrist and wrapped her into his arms. "You okay?" He talked into her hair, slick as flyline. "Want me to drive you? No students for an hour." His small fly shop in the converted garage offered fly tying and fly casting classes, and guided fishing trips during the various seasons.

"Sure, my head's in a crusher." Shelly leaned back, squeezed out a low voltage smile. "Aspirin will fix it."

During the fog-shrouded drive into town she rested her head against the cool window, silent. Skip wondered if this drizzle marked the start of the fall rains. *Kinda late this year.* He was half past ready to throw at some salt-fresh salmon, sea lice still clinging to their strong sides. Get some trips booked. Yeah. He thought about what Shelly said—it took him back a ways.

Freckles, their eight-week-old German Shorthair puppy. Rubbery-legged, with a gray steer belly that smelled like hay, and envelope-flap ears of heavy chocolate satin. But not a single freckle.

One warm spring Sunday they took him into the Sierras, where Skip fly-fished for golden trout—small, stained-glass fish in little streams edged by wild iris, soft grass, and buttercups. Freckles and Shelly explored deer and rabbit trails, then flopped, exhausted, in the cushiony grass to watch him play and release the red-gold trout. At lunchtime Freckles ate puppy food while they munched sandwiches. He curled up in the soft flowered meadow to nap as butterflies showed off their stiff, blue-powdered wings, dancing among the blossoms.

That night Freckles retched up mouthfuls of foam. Shelly called the vet.

"Give him a teaspoon of pepto and bring him in tomorrow."

They awoke to find Freckles dull-eyed and nauseous. He burped foam. They gave him another sip of pepto before Skip hurried to work. "See ya, hon, take care of the little guy."

Shelly had tried.

She quickly pulled on jeans and shirt, gathered purse and keys, called work, and hurried to bundle up Freckles.

He had crawled off his blanket and spit up on the bathroom floor. She dampened a towel, crouched down, and carefully wiped his foam-flecked muzzle. He quit breathing. Stunned, she lifted him, blew dainty puffs of air into his tiny black puppy nose, pressed his small gray tummy. Puff, puff. Press. She begged, "Oh, please, breathe." Cadence. Puff, press, beg. But he lay still and soft and silky in her arms. After an eternity she swaddled him in his blanket like the baby he was, and wiped sheets of tears off her cheeks.

She called Skip.

"I'll be right there. You okay?"

"No."

Shelly slumped on the sofa while Skip phoned the vet. "Well what do you *think* it was? He didn't last long enough!" He used the edge of anger to scrape away his pain. "Yeah, I guess. Yeah, I will. Bye." He hung up hard. Watched Shelly twist a tissue. "Said puppies sometimes get a bad hit of distemper or parvovirus and there's nothing anyone can do. . . ." His face defined glum. "Damn, I don't like it either, hon."

"It's not fair, he didn't even have a chance to be a big dog." She sniffled.

Skip squeezed her hand. "What short life he had was perfect as any puppy's."

They pampered their animals without shame. Shelly's Dad joked about it, said next lifetime he wanted to be reborn as one of their dogs. She nodded, sighed, worked out a grin but it fit crooked. "Guess I'll get to work."

"Let me take you, if you're ready."

"No, I really need to walk."

That was when she noticed—it. She walked the half-mile to work most days, even in the snow. The air would clear her head, she reasoned. But doorstep to office, despite frequent stops to sniff carnations and sweet peas that crowded through picket fences, she had smelled something, well, weird. It seemed to emanate from inside her nose, her very neurons. A strange, dry, pungent, illusion of a scent, drier than old paper, more ancient than frankincense. It puzzled her, lingered through repeated splashes of cold water, hovered within her the entire day.

Into her stillness Skip said, now, "Are you sure it was the same smell?"

Shelly's eyes widened, as if he had just stepped out of her mind. That heavy, dry pungency without origin clung to her again with its haunting echo of life. She suspected what it meant. "Yes."

At three o'clock she answered the office phone, routinely. Answered The Call. Her voice gargled through the clutch in her throat when she relayed it to Skip.

They sped up the scenic highway—narrow, winding, and dangerous—where steep wooded hills plunged to a rocky shoreline inhabited by sea lions, puffins, and auklets. Endless green waves crashed into foam and sent an iodine-scented mist swirling up through pines and rhododendrons; in spring the dark forest would blossom with patches of bright pink beauty. Shelly stared at the strip of pavement in front of them. Skip knew she needed to face the truth she had resisted all year, but he didn't know how to help. Impossible to avoid reality now, to pretend a miracle would happen and her Dad would be well again.

"Talk to me?" he hoped aloud.

She growled her throat clear. "Thinking. About this log cabin by a lake, Mom and Dad on a fishing vacation. Wondering where they found a bakery in those mountains to bake my pink birthday cake. About when he ran, it must have been *miles,* alongside me in the summer sun, while I learned to ride my first bike. How surprised, when I noticed he'd long since removed his hand from the fender." Shelly weighed the patience that gentle deception revealed. The sacrifices required, difficulties overcome to provide a new blue sweater, a birthday puppy. "Daddy's girl, Mom always said." True then, still true.

Skip smiled, listened to the thrum of tires on the pavement, the snip-snap as the wipers cleared a soft briny mist from the windshield.

Shelly went on. Into the battle now. She admitted her refusal to loosen her grip, railing against the darkness as if willpower could magically win the favor of her father's return to health. Vibrant again, fishing with Skip, telling his stories. Hot shame prickled her skin. Her strong bond to these cedar-scented hills, thundering seas, and fish-thickened streams should smooth her acceptance of the rhythms of life. But not when it struck home. Not when ebb and flow meant someone she loved, gone. As if immunity from the laws of nature might be granted.

"Kinda hard on yourself," Skip upheld.

"I won't grow up any younger."

Skip gripped the steering wheel, negotiating the narrow curves in the first velvet light of dusk. He felt Shelly's turmoil. Tough, inescapable, this loss that faced them, everyone. He didn't know what to say or how to console her; words seemed hollow compared to her solid anguish.

"Have I acted awful . . . ?" her voice trailed to wistful.

"Of course not. Just quieter than usual. Until now."

The steady uphill grade of a coastal headland, thickly shadowed in green-black forest, reminded Skip of an all-time favorite fishing trip. Gem-filled creeks and hummingbird canyons, elk tracks in the mud. That time when Ben showed them around the rugged mountains where he and Shelly's mom had panned for gold, for wages, their first summer of marriage. A real adventure. Yeah. "Remember Idaho?" he prompted.

"Campfire smoke in my hair, our lumpy sleeping bags—it was wonderful. And those gorgeous, wild mountains he watched." Ben's tales of smoke-jumping throughout the remote forests near Canada had thrilled them with visions of danger and loneliness. He had ventured, known fear, danger, the unusual. Welcomed life's infinite variations.

"That's where you get it." Skip understood the root of her wanderlust, her restless urge to see the next town, mountain, country. A legacy of spirit. He knew she yearned to relish the wonders of a tropical rain forest, before they all disappeared; to swim in turquoise seas over coral reefs; to smile at gaudy fish. And Skip damn sure itched to fish for the Big Three, tarpon, bonefish, and permit. Ease across those heartbreak blue flats, the sun like a torch on your skin. Yeah. In his fly shop he had even tied a few of the fancy leaders, Bimini twists and all. He had fiddled around with some crab flies and Clousers, Black Deaths, and Cockroaches, hoping—just in case the chance ever arose. . . . Well, they would go. Before too late ended their chance.

Shelly announced, "We shouldn't wait."

Skip glanced at her, then back at the treacherous road. "You reading my mind?"

"About our dreams? What do you think?" She lifted her chin to peer down the cliffs, into the reassuring pulse of ocean swells. The truth sparkled clear as the waters of that salmon stream, a year ago. What drove the salmon drove them all. The cycle would continue. She wouldn't let her Dad down.

Despite their grim mission Skip felt cheered from the note of determination in Shelly's voice, a trace of her customary spunk. Already trying to cope, making plans. The setting sun created rainbow auras in the salty mist; it reminded him of that fable about rainbows and promises. He made one. "I think you're right—let's do it. You'll see your angelfish, I'll catch a tarpon."

After a moment she added, "I wonder if Mom would want to learn to snorkel."

Skip chuckled at the unlikely thought of Shelly's Mom putting aside a half-knitted afghan and hopping into the sea. But why not? He smiled encouragement.

Without warning a large, black cormorant swooped low across the darkened road. Strangely displaced in the twilight, as it should have been roosting far below on the jagged cliffs, it slammed under the wheels of their truck.

Skip's heart stuttered, Shelly gasped, "No!" and the shock of knowledge crashed through them—a taste of copper, a feathered broken scent in the rattle of silence. Shelly understood, and braced herself. Time had run out for the hapless bird; time had run out.

THREE

 *Tarpon Pilgrim*

"Good morning!" The tarpon guide hails my arrival. "You must be Jill Dunn. I'm Skip." He hums with barefoot energy, his face burnished from the sun.

"Yes, pleasure, morning," I yawn. It's not yet seven as I shuffle toward the wooden dock, the dense warmth of the salt air forming dew on my skin. Pink streaks brighten the Florida dawn like neon on wet pavement.

"How many we going to catch?" I try to act alert, but I barely slept last night. Too excited. I take a giant step onto the clean, graceful skiff. Across to a different world—deck underneath, not concrete. My balance struggles for center.

Skip's chapped lips split into a grin. "Depends. Your first tarpon trip, right?"

"How did you remember that?" I booked him last January. But maybe the pastel fishing duds mark me a rookie. Maybe we all look alike.

"First time, people think about numbers," Skip says. He stows my gear bag, agile, enviable. Then he leans down to swab up a couple footprints from the deck.

My face burns. I sneak a look at the soles of my reef shoes and find more dirt. Clever. Not a good idea to piss off your guide if you hope to catch fish.

He hands me the towel for my feet. "People think how many, what'll they weigh. More to it than that, though. You'll see. Ready?"

"Oh, yeah, just a sec." Perched on the cushioned seat, grateful for my new tidiness, I feel pale as a slug, swollen and oafish, awkward away from the shelter of my office, my car, my recliner. A poster child for the need to get out more. Well, this is it. Three whole days to try for a fly-caught tarpon. A passion grown from seed—planted by the first brook trout that rose to my McGinty. Winter evenings and videos did the rest. I bend over toward the rod rack. "Wait, I forgot to ask. Do I have the right fly on?"

Skip pauses to check my rigged outfit, the Cockroach I tied myself, gleaned from a book. "Nice tie. That'll work, unless you want to try one of mine."

Of course I want to try his, and say so—he's on a first-name basis with these fish, up on the hottest patterns. He hands me a muted blue and mottled brown creation from his stretch box, with translucent red eyes and a finely graduated hand-knotted leader. "Wow, what do you call this?"

"Tarpon Crab," he says, "Moves so good in the water you hardly need to work it."

I dandle it in the water a moment and watch fur and feathers become pulsing, swimming fish food. "Thanks, this is great."

He smiles and puts the boat in gear. "Better hold on to your hat when we clear this channel." His salty cap goes over the throttle control.

Mine comes off. "This has to be a great life," I babble as we idle out the canal. I mean it. The air smells tangy and thick with a faint wood scent, while brown pelicans with downy yellow heads and round blue eyes stand on battered pilings like honor guards.

He grins again, as if the keeper of secret knowledge. "Some days. This one looks good, maybe they'll be chewing. Ready? Hang on, we're going to blow and go."

My hand grips a rail as the skiff leaps up on plane. The wind pushes my cheeks toward my ears, and behind my polarized glasses tears leak from my eyes. We scream across water like gray silk toward a place in the distance only a guide could see. No horizon. Clouds and small wooded islands suspend in a stainless mirror, gateway to an alternate reality. A visual echo. Must be easy to get lost out here—what does he use for reference points? The expanse is awesome. It sets free a vague insecurity and dim memories, rumors of piracy, soak into my thoughts. When we stop I glance around to see why. It looks much the same as water we've crossed.

"We'll try it a while here," Skip says. He removes the long graphite pushpole from its clips on the gunwale, climbs onto the poling platform. "Better get ready."

My wandering mind pulls back, caught staring through invisible water at big umber goblets that mushroom from the turtle grass. "Oh, right. Earth to angler, heh, heh." I unrack my rod and lurch to the casting deck. In full tentative. My feet are wet cement, on backwards, and everything moves—the boat, the water, the clouds. The quiet presses in so hard my ears roar. My lame comment earns a chuckle from Skip.

"Those are cup sponges, good habitat for baby crustaceans, which tarpon love. We're going to pole this edge a bit, Jill. You work out some line and look for fish, okay? They'll be along right up here."

Sweat pops out on my hands and my arms fit like some-one else's—some uncoordinated wimp's. The worry that I've forgotten everything I never knew emerges. "What do I look for?" My voice croaks, my straining eyes search the water for a target.

"They're hard to miss. Big dark moo-moos. Keep the fly in your line hand, ready."

"Oh, sure." Had they told me that at the saltwater fly-fishing school?

"Remember to keep your feet still so you don't step on your line."

Yeah, I remember that. "And bow to the fish, right?" A rush of gratitude floods through me as my brain resumes operation.

"First we've got to get you hooked up. Let me see you cast."

A few false casts and out one goes—not my best, but fair. Although newly purchased last winter, the twelve-weight has become familiar from hours of practice, ruining fly lines on my lawn. I strip in the line and peek back at Skip, there on the tower like a judge, a monument. He probably thinks that looked pathetic.

"Okay. Good to see you've put in some time. See that patch of grass about ten o'clock? Try one five feet to its left."

I go all warm from the crumb of recognition, but now it's accuracy time and the clumsies strike again. My elbows mutate into clubs. It takes a major effort to discipline my-self and wing one out.

"Not bad. A bit short, but that's better than lining 'em."

Smugness reigns. This isn't so hard! *Novice breaks world record*, the headlines read in my fantasy-filled head.

We glide along, the pushpole dripping water, an occa-sional soft "uh!" from Skip the only sounds. The tiny movements of the skiff seem less noticeable now. The sun has lifted in the sky and sweat is soaking my hatband. I'm tired of standing. My feet hurt. I look at my watch—only twenty minutes have passed.

"Jill! Eleven o'clock! Two hundred feet!"

My heart stops beating and my eyes catch fire. "I see them! I see them!" Huge torpedoes come toward us, too big to be fish. Their size holds menace. Can I handle it if I hook one? Better check my line, see that it's not tangled.

"Good. Good," Skip says. Then, "Get ready. Only a couple false casts. Pick your fish, try for one on the edge of the school. Okay, now!"

I go for it, despite the buzz of static, the gray confusion in my skull. One, two, three. . . .

"Lay it down!" Skip yells.

My cast booms forth. It twists in the air, piles into a bird's nest and whacks the lead fish in the head. Tarpon turn themselves inside out, churning the water like an exploding hand grenade. I crawl up from a pit of despair and strip in line, imagine donning a concrete life vest and ending this ruined life.

"You'll need to lead 'em a little more than that," his brevity is a welcome kindness.

Okay, missed a shot. Toughen up, do better. Better doesn't happen. Not on the next cast, when I smack the side of the boat and roll the hook point into a spoon. Nor the one after that, when I yank the freshly sharpened Tarpon Crab out from the lips of an eager fish. The day wears on, wearing me down. Why hasn't Skip choked me? It would be a relief compared to this dismal and crushing display of incompetence. Did I really think it would be easy to waltz in off the trout stream and take on these big boys?

"Here they come! High and happy!"

"I'm on 'em! I'm on 'em!" My flabby arms burn from casting but they do it again. This time the line turns over, settles the fly neatly in front of a tarpon the size of a Holstein. Moo-moo indeed. None of the others spook. I freeze, mindless, paralyzed. What happens now?

"Strip! Strip!"

Oh yeah. I strip fly line and watch the tarpon. Forever. Armored with impossible silver, his eyes seem enormous. Then my heart beats again.

"Slow it down, Jill! Mess with his head! *Make* him eat!" Skip yells, coaches, directs, pleads.

The urgency of his voice steers my hands and connects me to the fly that scoots, scoots in front of the big-jawed face. The tarpon's back glows deep cobalt blue and now he's close to the fly! He surges forward and a jolt shocks my arms.

"Hit him! He's got it! Hit him! Clear your line!"

My line hand jerks on automatic pilot. An electric throbbing jerks back. His strength is incredible. My knees quiver and I wonder if my hair has turned white. I hit him again. Fly line swirls around me like spaghetti in a blender, then zings out the guides of the rod. My reel starts to sizzle.

"He's coming up! Bow! Bow!"

My limbs obey but don't know it. I hunch over the front of the boat and the most beautiful thing in creation hurtles out of the glassy water and stands on his tail. He must be six feet if he's an inch! Blinded by the reflection of sunlight on scales, goosebumps wave over my skin. I'm hooked to this dazzling creature and there's no letting go.

The tarpon, my tarpon, twists like a gymnast, then craters back down. Foam erupts around him and a whoosh of brine reaches my nostrils. I smell the essence of life in its rich soupy tang. I feel strong and weak, full, complete. He accelerates suddenly, riveting my attention; how can the huge creature move so fast? He greyhounds into the blue-green, streaking toward the imagined safety of deeper water, way into the backing before I can blink.

"Put as much heat on him as you can," Skip pants.

I glance back and see the pushpole bent into an arc as he leans his whole body into it, shoving the skiff after the retreating tarpon. The chase begins.

My tarpon leads us further, further. I try to follow Skip's instructions. "Pump and wind, keep the line tight, don't let him rest," and such, all in hoarse gasps as he humps the boat forward. I feel a bruise form on my stomach where the rod butt is jammed, and my elbows begin to tremble. A hot band of pain has replaced my back. I re-evaluate my understanding of strength. This fish *owns* strength. I want to touch him, share his power. My cramped reel hand renews its efforts and the spool gains some line. The tarpon jerks it back. I groan, and Skip cheers me on. I feel like I've been fighting this fish forever. Maybe longer. Somehow I'd never pictured fly-fishing as an endurance test—real physical struggle, real sweat. If I'd known I would have trained, run marathons, pumped iron. I had underestimated my quarry.

"He's getting tired," Skip says.

How can he tell? Tired? Compared to what? I'm ready to collapse, give up, retire to a hammock and an adventure novel. Leave the tough stuff to superheroes. Then I see him, my tarpon. Closer now, he turns sideways and my throat swells over a lump of awe. His gill plate seems sculpted metal, his look charged with alien experience.

"Give him the down and dirty," Skip urges.

Blood roars in my ears as I work the rod, going low, going left when the fish goes right, going low again. I make promises to gods I don't know, promises to be worthy, if only I'm granted this one wish. Bargains, deals, sacrifices.

I taste salt on my mouth but can't tell if it's sweat or I've bitten myself. It doesn't matter. This fish matters. I pump and reel.

Skip calls out, cautioning me. "Remember Jill, he might blow up again when he gets near the boat."

I grunt acknowledgement and shift my weight to relieve spasms in my legs. A force of living current pulses up the line and I crackle with tension. He's Up. A molten pillar of head-shaking, gill-rattling drive for freedom confronts me. I stand dazed, Midwest face to Megalops face, seeing through the looking-glass. Skip yells but I don't understand. Tarpon rapture fills the breathless vortex. So quick, so silver, he descends, tips away, returns to his world. Crashes across the leader.

He's off.

Free from the strain, a short ess of line snaps back, lashing me. I gasp and Skip groans.

It's over.

And I'm different. Changed, older. Weary, from the most intense hour of my life. But way past happy. "Wow," I understate. "I see what you mean."

"Thought you would," Skip says. He sits on the poling platform and mops his face with a blue bandanna. "These fish get to you." Then he stands up, saying, "Ready for the next one?"

"The next one," I repeat, no longer the same clueless newbie greenhorn. Now when the folks back home talk tarpon I'll smile and nod wisely. Sympathize with their tarpon-battered arms, ruined backs, bruised bellies. Describe how *my* silver king jumped, how much line he took, how he dazzled in the sun.

Now I know why the guides say, "Bow."

FOUR

PART I: ASPIRATION

Post-nuclear public buildings. Skip flashed on them first thing, at the border crossing. He hoped a movie producer or two would capitalize on this asset, save themselves a bundle on set construction when they cast apocalyptic films, like "Fort Barracuda, LA," or whatever.

He braked the truck, opened Shelly's door. "Guess this is us."

They needed tourist permits to explore the tarpon fishing in Mexico, and so had dutifully followed the arm waves of a well-padded man in a tan uniform to this huge, modern structure with ornamental frescoes on its exterior walls. Snakes and birds. No fish symbols evident. Piles of rubble about. The place emitted a fragmentary air—Skip thought he could smell wet cement.

Inside loomed a vast, empty space with two clusters of men, balanced, one at each end. Guessing, Skip and Shelly marched toward the group to their right, and presented their birth certificates to a serious-looking man behind a narrow counter. He wore a neat clipped mustache and leather belted uniform like an actor in a movie. Lots of braid. Behind him, where normally you would expect an office cubicle complete with desks and telephones, a plump bun-haired *señora* in shapeless calico cooked the noon meal on a compact grill. The good smells, like Shelly's chili, with dueling whiffs of refried beans and *comino,* made Skip's stomach growl. It looked as if their office supplies consisted of three pens and a stamp pad on the counter. And fresh *tortillas*.

Shelly spoke some words in Spanish and the actor man smiled and stamped two pieces of paper, which he handed them.

"How's it going?" Skip felt uneasy.

"*Perfecto,*" she grinned. "Gave us a hundred and eighty days. Ought to find some tarpon by then."

They clomped across the gray concrete floor of the echo chamber to the other knot of men. A single ancient manual typewriter decorated that counter. A twin of the first man used it to peck out letters, haltingly typing entries onto their documents. A couple phones served that side of the "office," but the predominant feature remained the abundance of manpower—maybe two dozen strong in the big, otherwise empty, building. A table stood nearby covered with piles of papers in what appeared total disorder. No filing cabinets. Skip realized it must take hordes of people to accomplish anything, what with their lack of equipment and all.

The second actor smiled, spoke, and gave over their permits. Shelly said, "Now they have to look at our stuff."

Skip's stomach fluttered with a pang of nerves. He hadn't spent much time in Mexico except for shopping excursions with Shelly into carnival-like border towns. Gear-ing up to spend a long time, months, maybe more, south of the border had given him a lot of what-ifs to ponder. He had thought, wanted to think, mostly about what kinds of flies to tie to catch tarpon. Cockroaches, streamers, important thoughts like that. He pictured himself on sparkling azure water, the air balmy and filled with clatter of coconut fronds and scent of mangoes. Strings of great-scaled, majestic tarpon would glide within range of his small boat, and his angler would cast—and he and Shelly would live happily ever after on his humble but adequate tarpon guide earnings. He had wondered quite a bit about snook, too. But other details had demanded attention, like storing left-behind belongings and buying insurance for their truck—a jolt of sticker shock that had left them feeling halfway mugged.

Now that they had passed the first stage, accepted as little apparent threat to the future of Mexico, he worried how snoopy these guys would get. He could imagine their expressions if they opened boxes of his fly-tying materials: the whole spectrum represented by piles of feathers, yarn, tinsel, and fur. He fretted that certain items might be forbidden; he hoped nothing illicit lurked in his trunk. Tales of Mexican jails made legendary campfire horror stories.

Four smiling, uniformed, and uniformly mustached men crowded around the rear of their truck. They acted as if they would truly love to see every item that it had taken Skip the better half of yesterday to wedge into the back—his personal jigsaw puzzle in three dimensions. A Fishing Life.

"Okay, now," Shelly whispered to him.

Skip turned into his awkward twin. Like walking backward blindfolded. In his world you could visit jail for doing this—and learn to enjoy the view. Shelly had explained, with her customary great patience, that if he *didn't* go along, they might get hassled. For not following the custom. "Try to think of it as similar to a campaign contribution," she had reasoned.

So he retrieved the sheaf of fivers from his jeans and doled them to the mustachioed guys, with considerable hilarity at each other's versions of each other's language. Skip had floundered in Spanish class, he thought partly due to the crone teaching that course. Cranky woman would snap her fingers at students like they were trained dogs expected to bark, and wear the same rancid dress days in a row. He could detect that stench even from the back row, where he scrunched low to avoid his name being called. So when he handed a five to the final recipient of graft he needed Shelly's help. "What did he say?"

"Give only one dollar to the small, older man with the gray mustache."

Gray Mustache busily fussed over sealing their suitcases with a paper tape that declared all contents safe and acceptable to this Republic. Skip questioned the financial disparity, but followed Shelly's direction.

The older man accepted his dollar slowly, with a look of surprise. As if he'd just dropped onto the planet. He said, in his fractured English, and with a tone of profound innocence, "For me?"

That did it—caught off guard, Skip couldn't help but crack up. He burst into a sneeze of laughter. Not only from the tension of trying to make himself understood, but also from this old guy's air of incorruptibility amidst a scene of clear and simple bribery. Shelly started giggling, then they all joined in. These gringos will laugh at the funniest things.

After handshakes all around, and almost floating with relief, Skip put their truck in gear and they headed south.

"Can we make Tampico tonight?" he asked.

"Maybe. That took longer than we planned."

"Yeah. Guess we better get used to it."

The drive brought contrasts that hooked into Skip's imagination. They rolled across a semi-arid agricultural plain, bypassing sparse hamlets of shelters built from vertically bound sticks and roofed by palm frond thatch. With TV antennas. Kids and dogs watched pregnant women in faded dresses sweep dirt in barren yards. More upscale settlements boasted homes with corrugated tin roofs, or cinder block walls. Several round, white-washed homes with neatly clipped thatch won Shelly's vote for beauty, their mutual favorite being one of those English cottage clones that sported a satellite dish.

By the time they passed their first turnoff, after undergoing an unexpected inspection by a military outfit toting full automatics, Skip had learned, "A lot of things they don't mention in travel guides."

Shelly said "mm hmm" in fervent agreement as she balanced her Spanish dictionary on the dash and consulted a map.

Now Skip understood where the *mañana* thing might have originated. For one, it took at least twice as long as they had allowed going anywhere. Then you had to take into account all the people who wanted to check you out, make sure you held properly stamped *papeles*. Also, even though they hummed along over some smooth and well-paved roads, other roads, for long stretches, would make a tire dealer think he had found heaven. All that divot-hampered forward progress made for a distinctly hesitant accelerator foot. Plus you had to deal with obstructions caused by huge, stinky fuel trucks, crawling up hills in front of them at a bristling ten miles per hour. He dared not try to pass on the narrow, winding, unlit mountain roads. So he drove on in spite of the oncoming darkness, although a little freaked by those legendary tales of *bandidos* who wait in shadows for dumb *yanqui* tourists to plunder. As if they had a choice, anyway, stuck there behind Juan Pemex.

By the time they finally arrived at the relative safety of a motel parking lot in Tampico, Skip and Shelly had convinced themselves that the only real dangers encountered had been those huge craters that jumbled their lane of highway. Okay, add in the beat-up clunkers, full of happy *campesinos* chugging toward town, without lights of any kind. The clunkers would pop suddenly from a vault of gloom, about ten feet beyond range of Skip's headlights. Fenderless relics held together by refried beans and hope, they made for a thrill or two. And cows. Sleeping on the pavement. Nice, warm smooth pavement. When the occasional vehicle approached, it didn't appear to bother these animals greatly. They propped themselves on their knees, haunches high, struggled to stand, then lumbered away with a dignified totter. Of course, that wasn't often, because most people had better sense than to drive after dark in these parts. Yeah.

Skip blamed himself for part of the delay, though. He had chosen to look over a lagoon that had beckoned to him from the map, named Laguna Madre. It shouted good habitat. They had found a tiny village at the seaside end of a long, winding, and muddy road downhill. La Pesca, name like that, had to be fish there, right? Maybe a dozen houses with minimal amenities filled the tiny grid of the village.

At a small wood-floored store that sold hot cokes and children's lacy Sunday dresses in yellow and pink, a plump friendly lady said—in Spanish to Shelly—"Yes, they had heard of the fish called tarpon. No, she didn't know anything about any boney-fish. Mostly the men there, they worked at a big shrimp farm the government built, up the lagoon, or they netted fish for market." The N word.

Skip's mood thudded. Though maybe the onset of a January drizzle added its influence.

"Should we try to find a place here?" Shelly had asked. "It's getting late."

Skip shrugged, looked around. Rain-soaked clouds and lowering light. Didn't look like this tiny burg had a motel. But Shelly spoke more with the store lady and walked across the street with her, and alongside a house. Skip stood there sipping his hot coke, feeling out of touch.

Shelly returned, shaking her head. While they headed back up the mud slick one-laner, she told him the lady had offered to rent them a "spare room" for the night. It consisted of a shed in her backyard, with one unglazed, unscreened, wood-shuttered window the size of a newspaper and two bunks covered by army blankets. A dirt floor. Shelly had gracefully declined.

"Guess what else," she said, releasing a sigh. "I asked her more about what fish they catch in the nets and she told me they sometimes get tarpon in them, but they sell them for fertilizer. Sorry."

Skip hit the bummed out bottom. These folks had a ways to go, it seemed. Someone needed to let them know the great value those gorgeous air-breathing silver fish held as a lure to sport fishermen, much more so than helping Joe Suburbanite feed his roses. Compare the pennies to the pound rose food to the countless dollars fishing tourists would spend on guides, lodging, food, and local handicrafts. Sacrilege, a crime, to even think of those awesome creatures treated with such a lack of respect. Skip's catch-and-release heart raged at the transgression. "Damn us humans. We just don't get it," he grumbled.

Shelly stared out at the gray mist.

Halfway uphill toward the highway they spotted a more believable motel, unnoticed in their prior rush to the sea. It had six rooms, clean tile floors, and real sheets on the beds. But Skip's nerve endings tingled, signaling wariness and uncertainty. Four rooms were already rented to local working men who hunkered in groups alongside the parking area, right out in full drizzle, cooking their evening meal on a sheet of tin that they had propped over coals. Shelly called it a *comal*. They acted friendly enough. But Skip insisted that he felt, well, like a hippy in a redneck bar.

"Culture shock," Shelly said.

"Hmm," Skip grunted in reply. He thought of himself as more sophisticated than that. Not like he had lived his whole life and never left his backyard. But talking second-hand through Shelly gave real meaning to cumbersome. Hard to tell what was going on. He wished now he knew more Spanish than "*otra cerveza, por favor.*"

Still, most of the highway signs bore that universal pictograph style, so even though some looked strange to his eyes, all but a few of them had begun to make sense. ALTO was common enough, easy to figure out that it meant STOP. But what the hell did TOPES mean?

"Watch out! Speed bumps," Shelly blurted. She admitted to some pressure, too. "My brain's about to explode," she said after deciphering another sign for him. "It's been so long since I used any Spanish, the two languages have tangled up in my head."

Early the next day Skip became familiar with the myth of unleaded gasoline. He had read in a travel guide that it often proved harder to locate than in the States. How about harder to find than the Lost Dutchman's Mine? He felt baffled, thwarted to a degree he had formerly encountered only after his thousandth futile cast at a lock-jawed North Umpqua steelhead. Sure, they saw "Extra" pumps at well-spaced Pemex stations. *Pero no, señor*, we have no "Extra" in the pump. Helpful citizens, eager to please, assured him, *sí, señor*, there is "Extra" at a station near the edge of town. They supplied careful directions. Skip's hopes would soar. They would find their way, spot a lonely silver pump at one end of the row and drive right up to it, only to have their worst fears confirmed. *No, señor*, we have no "Extra" in this pump. He began to wonder if they exported it all, or maybe it marked a weekly or monthly event. The Big Day, the arrival of unleaded. Parades, floats, *mariachi* bands. He wondered how long their truck would last, running on this low octane, leaded stuff they were forced to use. He wondered about his sanity. Now he knew why they saw so many diesel-powered vehicles.

Skip would learn as the days wore on Many Things He Wished He Had Remembered About Diesel. Diesel engines make abundant racket. All the buses and trucks they saw run on diesel. Numerous buses and trucks clog Mexican cities. They run all night. A fact that had somehow escaped their attention, lulled by the quiet evenings spent in their Tampico motel. That place, just like home, even offered TV. Skip loved one station that showed old Hollywood movies with Spanish subtitles. He had watched *Jaws* closely in an effort to enlarge his vocabulary. *Tiburón*.

Puttering down to, and all around Tampico, Skip also had ample opportunity to reflect on how widely driving differed in Mexico. The simple act of moving from one location to another became a whole new experience. One of the first issues that rose like a trout to a Muddler, turned out—no Rest Stops. *Nada*. So if either he or Shelly missed their chance at relief back at the greasy Pemex station while filling up with crappy gas, and taking turns

to watch their truck, and making sure whichever atten-
dant appeared put the numbers on the pump back to zero
before starting it, and keeping flocks of urchins (why
aren't they in school?) away, and wondering why not only
no bathroom tissue exists in the restroom, but frequently
no toilet seat, no lock on the door (which has no handle),
no soap, and usually no running water—if they passed up
that golden opportunity, the second big flash of awareness
loomed large—No Shoulders Edge These Roads. Even
Shelly, who didn't seem to have suffered much culture
shock at all, which added to Skip's uneasiness, gasped,
appalled, when a car stopped right on the road in front of
them and several guys spilled out of it and unbuttoned
themselves. Whizz. Right there. But after another few
miles an insistent pressure stripped away years of training and modesty.

Shelly sighed, "My teeth are begging for life vests."

So Skip stopped, right on the road, because, well,
where else could he go? Shelly ducked into a wall of leafy
bushes.

Driving worked pretty damn different in town, too. Co-
ziness ruled Tampico streets, as everyone tried to fit four
lanes of traffic onto a two-lane road. Taxicabs shunned all
decorum and kept two wheels on the sidewalk as much as
possible, stopping every few yards to cram one more person into an overloaded interior. Guys could give sardine
packers a lesson.

"How in the hell do they figure the fares?" Skip
commented.

And traffic lights. They presented a real challenge to
Skip's adaptability. Years of ticket avoidance had instilled
in him a reflex—to stop at a red light and remain until it
changed to green. Surprise. He found such behavior not
the custom in Tampico. Cars approached, stopped, and if

no imminent danger of collision hurtled toward them, proceeded. When Skip waited for a green light, horns started blasting. Crazy gringo!

Of course, locals ought to recognize by their out-of-country plates that Skip and Shelly didn't know the rules. But they had driven a couple days in wet weather, thereby achieving that fashionable in-country mud-toned look. License plate, windows, it blended into the road. Looked like a mud sculpin as much as a truck, from this artistic camouflage.

"What makes these roads so muddy?" Skip grumbled, dodging craters.

However, trucks, cabs, buses—one and all—stuck around patiently for the green at traffic lights where there stood a uniformed enforcer holding a submachine gun. While lingering at Stop or I'll Shoot Street, entertainment came for free, supplied by a madman with a jumbo cigarette lighter and a torch. He fired up and stuck the burning torch far enough down his throat to gag his mother. Shelly's eyes rolled over to Skip, but no escape appeared from this captive traffic circus nightmare. Urchins climbed up their fenders with squeegees and greasy rags, threatening to "clean" their windows. Skip didn't care, mud covered the things anyway; windows and urchins. Finally, the light changed, uniform tweeted his whistle, and they drove away, free from such depressing sights. Maybe they would make it down this Nightmare Avenue to that chicken place after all. *Pollo* Wonderful.

The food. Superlatives jostled in Skip's mouth, trying to win as the first one out. He found himself marveling at full, sweet flavors in everyday dinner rolls. *Bolillos* from paradise. Cheeseburgers could wait; he wanted to eat six of these. He exclaimed over a simple bowl of chicken soup with green leaves floating in it. "Cilantro," Shelly said, filling her spoon. Local beef, leaner and quite a bit less tender, tasted so savory that he reflected with dismay at those wasted years spent swallowing soft, tasteless cardboard supermarket meat. Even Shelly, whom he once suspected of being a closet anorexic, surprised him by cooing over smoky grilled chicken served with fresh corn tortillas and lots of chunky salsa. Snapper Vera Cruz appeared often on the menus, but Skip never ate fish. A matter of principle.

Before leaving Tampico they located a lagoon-side marina where they pursued further research. "I've got to see some water," Skip told Shelly at breakfast, so she rustled the map. Sunshine and salty air, nice modern buildings, unkempt grass, reached by a road that definitely looked as if it had experienced a bombing run. Huge holes gouged out of the pavement, in front of houses that could only be called mansions—two and three story, arched windows and doors, ornate grillwork everywhere, a canopy of massive tropical trees, festooned with orange and lavender blossoms.

Shelly asked about renting a boat with a guide, perhaps, to fish the lagoon. A pleasant lady, the sole person visible in the whole marina area, said "Yes, it could be arranged, a man would take them fishing for" what amounted to five dollars an hour. Skip thought that sounded like a damn good deal and a great way to determine what manner of fishing transpired hereabouts. He itched to drag out a fly rod and discover what would bite, but they needed to move on, just a little farther now.

Driving south they crossed a graceful steel bridge that spanned a mangrove-lined river. To the west as far as Skip could see stretched that huge lagoon, an estuary. Habitat for sure. It would bear checking out. But first they would continue to the farthest point south on their agenda. They figured that if they stayed within a day or two of driving time from the border, or a short trip from a major airport like Tampico, they could host fishermen from the States looking for tarpon. Find that legendary little villa, that inexpensive Mexican rent, have just enough fishing guests down to make a living. Yeah.

PART II: REALITY

The countryside grew more green, dense with tall grasses and trees with crimson flowers. They saw roadside stands with handpainted signs—*Coco Frío*—and country people leading burros pulling small wobbly carts. The highway continued to alternate between smooth and cratered, but widened for a long stretch. Skip relaxed. Felt himself getting into it.

As they neared Tuxpan they encountered rolling hills adorned with tracts of small brick homes. Solar panels on their roofs, curving streets, sidewalks, tidy yards. Nice. Skip had read in his guidebooks that the area south of Tuxpan represented a major winter destination for lots of *norteamericanos*, and that the Mexican government catered to them considerably. Going so far as sending out Green Angels, government trucks equipped with all manner of roadside automotive help, a free service to assist travelers. Keep those dollars flowing. They had passed several green trucks already, and Skip had started calling them Road Apples, which made Shelly giggle and ask why.

"'Cause they're green and all over the road," he quipped. Not to make fun of the service—he thought it an unusually civilized and kindhearted thing to do, especially considering that this country endured such extensive poverty. A ray of hope. If they could understand the con-

nection between these caravans of motorhomes, and pros-
perity, they could figure out the tarpon/fisherman thing.
Hell, some of those old farts driving motorhomes might
even be tarpon fishermen, or as Skip had discovered usually the case in the fishing "bidness," at least wannabe, po-
tential tarpon fishermen. Hell, yeah.

In Tuxpan, which Shelly told him meant "Place of the
Rabbits" in the indigenous tongue, they happened upon a
charming, spotlessly clean hotel overlooking a travel
poster scene of plaza and river. Skip parked their truck in
a locked and guarded lot, and they, well Shelly, checked in.

The broad marble stairway curved to the second floor
and out to a wraparound balcony. They chose a front
room with a romantic view, disdaining those viewless
rooms at the rear of the hotel, the ones with air conditioning. They spent a balmy winter evening ensconced on
the balcony, delighting in the impressive human spectacle
and lush postcard vista. Palm fronds slapped, red, pink,
and yellow flowers dotted bushes and trees, small boats
with twinkling lights ferried passengers across a wide blue
river to houses on the other side. Skip didn't see anyone
trolling, or even fishing from the shoreline. Downtown, of
course not, he reasoned. Families strolled around the
plaza, dressed in fine and vivid clothes with a faintly '50s
look. Dads in cardigan sweaters carried infants in ruffled
dresses. Moms in high heels and skirts held toddlers by
the hand. Children abounded. Young girls decked out as if
for a party wandered around in pairs and pretended not to
eye young guys sitting on benches. Hair slicked back,
wearing pointy black shoes and crisp white shirts, the
guys eyed them back.

Quaint, Skip thought, as cars and trucks decorated
with fringe or dingle balls around their windows rolled by.

Buses displayed ornate shrines on their dashboards, and had fortune cookie religious mottoes painted on their colorful diesel-powered rears. He and Shelly retired into the tropical night, their ceiling fan doing its duty, wafting noxious fumes right to their noses, while ceaselessly shifting gears from the street below kept them tuned in to their environment. They arose in the morning, queasy, heads splitting, and quite literally exhausted, but cheerful in the face of their foolish choice of room. Now Skip wouldn't forget about diesel.

They drove a kilometer or so down river to its outlet at the beach, looking for a clue to any fishing activity. They found a deserted yellow beach, palms, pines, and the turquoise Gulf of Mexico with its small surf. No people around to question, however haltingly. Skip thought maybe he should try casting into those guts between waves, see what bit. Use his 10-weight, in case a taker with some size to him came along, and maybe one of those bigger popping bugs. Everything fishy loved those suckers.

"Go ahead," Shelly said, grinning, even though Skip hadn't said a word. "I know you're going to explode if you don't make a throw or two here. I'll look through this." She had bought a paper to search the ads for rentals. She pulled her calculator out of her tote bag, found a suitable patch of sand, and spread the paper over her crossed legs.

Skip strung his rod and went for it. His first cast he hauled in a way over-gunned *mojarra*. Yeah, he knew that people fried 'em up and said they tasted good, but dinky food fish weren't his target. He saw several gulls crashing and dipping at the surface a ways down, and hurried to get a shot into their action. He was rewarded by a scrappy bar jack. And another, and another. Fun, but still. . . .

After a while he rejoined Shelly.

"Well?"

He shrugged. "Maybe it's not the right time for them here. Or maybe it's not the right place. I don't know. A barracuda broke me off. How did you do?"

She frowned. "Expensive."

"How much is expensive."

"As much as where we stored our stuff at the border in Texas, uh, Brownsville. I thought housing in Mexico was supposed to be a bargain."

Skip shrugged again. That was her purview, home. He concerned himself with how to scope out fishing opportunities. Help arrived later in town.

They strolled through the small friendly city and found a cafe filled with local folks having lunch. Consumed a couple sinfully delicious little sandwiches, *tortas* the menu read, stacked with ham and cheese and avocado, and wandered back toward the hotel. At the lobby Shelly stopped to inquire about banks, and, introduced by the concierge, began chatting with another guest. An affable Mexican man, he identified himself as Victor, from Vera Cruz, who had rented an apartment in the hotel while working on construction projects here. Thank God he spoke enough English that Skip could participate. Seeing them waver, unsure of his directions, he courteously offered assistance and drove them the few short but convoluted blocks right to the front steps of their destination.

Returned from their foray, they joined Victor for *cervezas* on the wide marble veranda. Shelly sat next to a potted hibiscus and sniffed the huge, pink trumpets of its blooms, wiped yellow pollen off her nose—blissed out on this sunny afternoon. Skip asked Victor if he knew anything about local fishing, or what species of fish were common to these waters.

"Not so much tarpon here," Victor told them, twinkling eyes green as the land of his Irish mother. "The river flows too fast, too fresh. They like that big lagoon just north of here, but no roads go to it."

"Yeah, I saw that one on the map. How can you get there?"

"By boat. Or maybe by donkey trail."

Skip felt frustrated, disillusioned by Victor's news. All this way and no fish? He didn't have the resources to man an overland burro safari to an unknown lagoon, dammit. If some folks operated on a shoestring budget, what he and Shelly worked with most people would call sewing thread. He pressed for more information.

The man explained, "Further south, tarpon *sí*, and off the beach, plenty of good fishing for many kinds of delicious fish. Did you try there?"

Skip nodded. "Not the ones I'm looking for."

"Did you see the big lagoon at Tampico?"

Skip nodded again, said he intended to check it out if nothing turned up down here.

"Ah, there my friend is Laguna del Chairel, the mother of all tarpon. I grew up on that water and it is full of those fish you're looking for. Also those with the stripe, the *robalo*."

All right! Progress.

They went for an exploratory drive south of town—thousands of shades of green, steep, pinched lanes through villages, thatched homes sprinkled over hillsides and peeking out from trees. Rivers, more hand-painted signs, these advertising vanilla, but no promising estuaries. Then they made a general ramble through residential sections of Tuxpan. Across the river seemed least expensive, Shelly said, but they found those streets narrow and unpaved. A blacksmith shop, *tortillerías,* and oily businesses that fixed tires scattered themselves among weathered two-story clapboard houses and sprawling stuccoed mansions surrounded by riotous tropical gardens.

"Let's head back toward Tampico tomorrow," Skip suggested. "Sounds like that's where we'll need to settle anyway. This place is beautiful, but it doesn't have that fishy feel, to me." He relied strongly on his instincts in that regard. The same subtleties of perception that cause a hunter to turn, to study a section of the woods just in time to catch the flick of a deer's ear. The senses that revealed which reach of stream would hold steelhead, and which would not. He kept thinking about what Victor had said. He wondered if they netted the tarpon up there, too. Victor hadn't thought so, but he hadn't lived on Laguna del Chairel for quite a few years.

They poked around the rest of that afternoon, exploring Tuxpan and looking for a place to enjoy a late lunch. They peered into storefronts where shiny new refrigerators and TVs sat displayed next to just-as-new treadle sewing machines and kerosene lamps. "New antiques," Shelly joked.

They walked to another plaza away from the river, flanked by a huge library that turned out as much a museum as a place for books. It smelled like history. Old leather and dust. They wandered through its two stories, admired glass cases filled with pre-Columbian artifacts of the Huastec and Totonac cultures. Numerous treasures came from *El Tajín,* an ancient city not far south. One of its last rulers had been named 13 Rabbit, which coincidence with the name Tuxpan amused Shelly. They admired clay pots molded into turtles and eagles, drinking cups with jaguar handles. Stone fishing weights shaped like various sized doughnuts. Feathered humanoid creatures that reminded Skip a little of the Hopi Kachina dolls he had seen in the American Southwest. Images straight from a peyote dream. He felt curious about what connections had existed between the civilizations.

A small street vendor stall a few blocks from their hotel beckoned to them with a delicious scent. Charring beef. Unpainted, weathered two-by-fours, spool table, battered metal chairs. There a tiny, skinny lady with long black hair and a clean white apron pressed tortillas by hand. The aroma from the grilled meat made them nearly faint with desire.

"*Carne asada*," Skip announced, proud to exercise a little language. "What do you think?"

Shelly smiled. "My mouth's watering. You know what they say about street stands though."

Yeah. Of course temptation won. They had traveled for days now, hogging out in absolute bliss in all the restaurants, feeling fine, confident. So what if a few flies buzzed around. It was outdoors, atmosphere, Skip rationalized. They ate grilled skirt steak, some variety of bean soup with cilantro and jalapeños, and round, golden mountains of the best tasting tortillas they had ever consumed.

"*Muy sabroso*," Shelly exclaimed to the small lady as she replenished their tortilla stack. They stuffed themselves so full that they waddled like fat ducks back to the hotel, in unabashed, culinary heaven. Skip felt like an alternate universe Jonah who ate the whale.

Gathering luggage the next morning, checking out, buying canned fruit juices for the drive north, Shelly radiated silence—too, too quiet.

"You all right?"

"Maybe."

Before they even arrived in Tampico her face wore a pale sheen. Skip could nearly see the fire of disease behind her eyes. After a couple attempts to find a less expensive hotel they gave up; none of them had secure parking near the rooms. A good portion of their life sat packed inside the truck. All Skip's fishing tackle. Too much to risk unguarded. Besides, Shelly looked as if she might pass out any minute, so they returned to their original motel.

Shelly, wobbling slightly, disappeared into the bathroom. For a long time. When she came out she fell onto a bed, shivering and pale. Skip covered her with a blanket and encountered the parameters of helplessness.

"What can I do? Anything?"

Murmuring weakly, "Call the desk, ask for a sealed bottle of *agua potable, purificada*, please."

He did. Felt pretty good, handling that situation. Met the guy at the door and everything. "Do you think this is from where we ate?" he asked her later, during a moment she seemed alert.

"Yeah. Must be."

"Then I'll get it, too? But I feel fine."

She looked at him with something like pity.

He went to the restaurant next door that evening, ordered himself a hamburger—*hamburguesa*. Shelly refused anything but water. They watched news on TV and Skip noticed the newscasters spoke so distinctly that he could almost understand more than every fifth word. The next day she stopped shaking so hard, so he brought her back some clear chicken broth and tea and toast. *Caldo de pollo, y té, con pan tostada*. Shelly would be proud of him, soon as she felt better enough to realize what he had done. Finally getting into it here, ready to find a little house and start fishing for a living. Yeah.

Later Shelly recovered enough to sit up, read the paper, look for a rental. "How do they afford it?" she exclaimed, leaning back, exhausted after tapping her calculator a moment.

"Whatever happened to those places we read about when we were back in the States where you could get a charming two or three bedroom adobe villa with a courtyard and garden for a buck and a quarter," Skip ranted. "Shit, throw in the maid and gardener and a couple parrots." He suddenly felt hot. Blurry. And when had one of those little burros kicked him in the gut?

What 13 Rabbit had in store for him ranked about as far from the civilized bouts of "upset tummy" that frequent TV commercials as a brain tumor from a tension headache. Shivering, flat on his back, aching in parts just discovered, Skip dreaded the next spasm that would send him crawling back to the porcelain temple. He gave thanks that Mexicans built large tiled bathrooms, since he now spent major blocks of time sprawled on the cool floor. Sometimes it was just too damn far back to bed. He berated himself for having done something so stupid, again. He wondered if the bottled water he sipped to stave off dehydration really was pure, or if it actually came from a tap and was only helping make him sicker. The lesson etched itself forever in his mind. From now on they would eat solely at restaurants, with refrigeration.

At times, feverish, clinging to his dream, he envisioned himself out on Laguna del Chairel, fishing for tarpon, the sun so hot it could bleach Pepsi. He saw the dark cobalt-bronze-green backs of tarpon rolling, seeming to play a mysterious fishy game as they circled each other in daisy chains. He saw himself cast from a crude *panga* to a cruising metallic beast at least his own size, saw its big grumpy mouth glom the Cockroach, saw it turn away unaware. He set the hook, hard, hard, and this tarpon, his tarpon, rose into the air in shock at the effrontery. A pillar of beauty, an icon of precious metal. Spanning the difference between their two kingdoms, forcing respect out of awareness. Not a nutritive meal for a rosebush, but a gleaming connection to Nature.

The weight of the heat in him twisted his thoughts into worry—had he done the wrong thing, those couple times he bought Shelly roses? Hell, now he could almost take pride in his deficiency in that department. Yeah, maybe he saved some tarpon by not buying roses. . . .

But again that giant creature claimed his inner sight, ruled his mind, as it thrashed up, out, punching free of the water, gill plates rattling. Great staring eyes, bright scales. . . . Flashed. Nova. Like a hole in the sun.

It broke him off. His fever broke.

He saw *Noticias* flickering on TV, something about California. He saw Shelly leaning against pillows by the phone, crossed-off classifieds in her lap, Shetland pony forelock brushing her eyelashes, her face stretched and pallid. She watched him, intently. As if he had mumbled strange words or . . . what? He thought about those street punks who had stolen the airstem caps from their truck while they rambled the central plaza in Tampico, jerks sitting there on the plaza wall with their oily sneers waiting for him to take the bait and get himself in a shitpot of trouble. He thought of Victor's generous assistance in Tuxpan, chauffeuring them, buying beers, explaining nuances, declining recompense. Contrasts. He felt a serious need for familiar ground, a place to regroup. He wondered if Shelly would hate him for not making this dream work out. For not becoming a tarpon guide. For not buying her enough roses.

He licked his cracked lips with a woolly tongue. "Hey, let's go home."

FIVE

Hold the Phone, There's a Bonefish on the Line

Skip hated to bitch. Usually. So what, apart from those violations named jet skis, would launch a Keys guide like himself into a rant? Well, when Florida Bay thunderheads sizzled and gale-force blasts drew foam lines in the shallows, for one What. Those days he'd have to wallow his skiff to the flats through heavy chop with whitecaps sudsing his teeth. By the time he arrived he felt as wrung and twisted as if he'd rode out the grunge cycle in a saltwater washer. Severe. But The Life kept him outdoors, which bulk of the year proved *no problema*.

Because, far as Skip was concerned, it was tough to match the sense of anticipation, the freedom, the Hunt involved, when poling across an oceanside flat. Scrunch, drip, scrunch came the subtle sounds from his pushpole, the skin-killing sun ablaze overhead, while his eyes strained, alert for telltale poofs from bonefish on a marl excavation. Bone spoor. Although they knew how to play dickhead and could turn harder to spot than zebras, bonefish rooting on the bottom tended to leave mud plumes, tracks as obvious as clouds in the sky to the observant bone stalker. Above, frigate birds with crimson throats and scissor tails would orbit over a sea the color of new jeans, and a smell like sargassum chowder would spread his lungs until his thoughts grew scaly logic.

Then you had to consider the permit. Magical mystery fish with their honed dorsals, curved and black, who would skim through the surface film as they moseyed alongside the boat. If he didn't know better (or did he?) he'd almost believe they copped a chortle or two at his expense. Because the minute he'd spy them and get all nutted up, calling out to his client to grab a rod, cast quick, they would zip away. Doubletime pronto, as if they understood more than any fish had a right to know.

Anyway, he could think better outside walls. Usually. Today his mental clarity suffered—no chance to jell between nagging interruptions. He was finally getting around to a second What worthy of a fishing guide's rant: phone calls. His angler *du jour* packed a cellular phone.

"Uh, Bill. Bill. If you'll point your rod toward ten o'clock, yeah, there, see the tails?"

Bill pointed his rod arm, a momentary statue, then with the other arm slipped his phone into a roomy shirt pocket. One of those nifty pastel shirts with gussets and mesh and noodles to hang things on and pockets big enough for fly boxes or wallabies. Maybe he'd been about to ring his broker, discuss his portfolio. Or return the call of one of the countless masses who had paged him, Out Here Fishing.

"Yeah, there. Give me a couple more strokes and I'll have you in range," Skip advised. Bill could see fish, a valuable, hell, priceless, asset in a flats fisher. One less obstacle to overcome, as flats fishing provides an ample degree of difficulty without flats blindness adding to the problem.

Another guide, a bud of his, once told a client he was so flats blind he should paint his rod white, with a red tip. Going for that repeat business. "Get ready now."

Bill found the Clouser minnow, held it in his line hand. He threw a decent loop when he fixed his attention on it, forgot about making phone calls and what a busy life he shouldered. A swirl of water, and twang, bonefish tails popped into sight like pewter erections.

"There, there, make the cast!" Skip stage whispered. Drab light today, one of those white skies that swallow contrast and thrash the local chamber of commerce into an agony of tooth-gnashing. Pretty damn hard to snap a postcard photo when dust blowing all the way from Africa bleached the subtropical sky to a chalky smear. As if to offset the tricky conditions, these bonefish had unknowingly cooperated by tailing, a fishy body of slime-coated flashers eager to expose themselves. A big one caught Skip's eye— so perpendicular to the bottom that his tail flopped wet against the quilted metal of his side. Bonezilla.

Bill delivered. His nine-weight settled the twig-sized fly smack in the path of the bonefish. Ready for them to discover. Perfect. Step right up, all you bones, and get your McClouser at the swim-through window.

Reeeeeeeennnnnggggg. The cellular jangled. Bill flinched. Skip swore. The bonespooks answered the call of survival. Bone fission.

"Sorry," Bill muttered, as he unfolded the vile object from his pocket. The tan Clouser lay on the sea bottom, abandoned.

Skip's heart rate hit full automatic, disappointment clashing with frustration. Guiding paid his bills—unlike some wild-mannered guides who fish for Team Grandma, content to live off their trust funds or x-mark calendars until those juicy bequests arrived. If his people compounded angler error to a stinky black-and-white payoff, well, it sure made it hard to get referrals from skunked fishermen. But he didn't know what more he could do, other than catch the goddam bonefish for them. He finds the quarry, sets the boat so the dude can pitch his maximum cast, coaches him on how to throw and when, and then—the phone rings.

The buzzwords gagged Skip: personal communications, global business, Keeping in Touch. How about stuff it up your personal globe. Okay, okay, sometimes instantaneous communication counted big time and was damn handy, even critical in certain situations. But in his creed, Fishing merited a Special Time, an interval set apart to dredge reality. Savor nature. How about even develop an Attention Span. Would it really pain anyone to risk stillness long enough to trigger a fresh thought? You could learn to key on the bonefish, how he roots for groceries, feel your muscle fibers, your beats as you cast, practice the taunting strips of your retrieve. It taxes a person's concentration to master such skills. It's not like fish want to be caught. To coax, to fool them with a hook masked in feathers and thread— that's communication, too. To trick a saltwater fish into chewing that fly like a starved moth devours your saddle hackle is way different than the toss, drift, mend, current- dictated result of a freshwater stream. Here the manipu- lation of the fly or lure rules the outcome. And either place, it's just not a cool time to check on the NASDAQ.

Bad enough to fritter away your lifecycle trapped in traffic behind some cellular junkie, watch his focus disin- tegrate while he hazards his beemer and your survival, but making those deals by god. Skip had seen one guy shaving, for chrissake. It wasn't a plague that affected just some clients and urbanites, either. He knew guides who'd be- come so enamored of their phones that they, too, punctu- ated every fishing trip with urgent calls. Not that his opin-

ions jibed with those numbnuts eager to return to the
grubby existence before penicillin and electricity. He realized that technology like his outboard, his phone, and his
computer provided him with crucial work tools. But for a
guy to drag a cell phone along on a fishing trip? If people
are that goddam busy why not just loll in their chilled hotel rooms and use the real phone and he'd idle into a marina now and then, punch their numbers, detail their romp
in the sun and catch ratio: "Yeah, they mudded good this
morning. I landed four out of six. Had lotsa fun. Want me
to send you the pictures?"

Hell, speaking of being unable to wrest oneself away
from the crush of modernity, once he'd fished a client who
lugged along his boom box. Skip stood, horrified, as the
guy hauled it out of a duffel. They had ranged to a legendary site on the Tarpon Trail where Skip staked the
boat. He knew that strings of migrating tarpon, like mute
submarines on a raid of grace, would float squarely to
whatever lucky angler stood on the bow. And then this
townie decreed that the moment, the day, The Experience,
would suffer without his music. Oh yeah. Boogie on Name-
free Bank. Before Skip could marshal wit one and cough up
a protest, his client had switched on and flooded the per-
vasive quiet with some do-wop elevator nightmare.

"Shut that damn thing off!" bellowed out from a skiff
that had tucked into second position. An old time guide,
one who Remembered When and who bore scant patience
with today's shriveling manners, echoed Skip's conviction.
The townie did, but not without cow eyes, as though Skip
should defend his presumed right to shatter the peace.
Deep into brain pain, shamed before a legend who had forgotten more secrets about guiding than Skip reckoned he'd
ever glean, Skip warned him, "You don't want to spook the
fish. Sound travels better under water than above."

The client had buckled and the pursuit of tarpon unfolded in accord with protocol. And consequently this client had hooked up. A chunky hundred-pounder powered skyward like a jet of metal blued whoosh, while saltwater ripped to foam. Sweat of arduous battle rimed the musical client's autographed shirt; his grunts of exertion the tunes Skip craved. Under a dragonfly sky, on a lime juice bay, and witnessing a duel of intents, Skip soaked up every wonderful nuance of the moment. He pushed the boat harder, faster, shouted "Bow!" and "Work that Rod!" and his angler heaved and reeled and flexed—until the alien sovereign neared enough to concede Optical Capture. The dazzle of the tarpon's gill plate shining like platinum, the sun beating with a ferocity more weight than heat . . . Skip knew the taste of fulfillment.

While Bill wound up his chat on the flat, Skip scanned the hydrous world in search of more bonefish. He wondered about his hydraulic steering, oozing ruddy fluid lately, its lifeblood draining away his ability to steer through sharp turns in the mangrove creeks. Maybe Bill could use his goddam cell phone to summon a towboat if it failed. Get the cartoon-like red one that resembled a tub toy. Yeah. He wolfed his ham-and-cheese on the tower so he wouldn't miss fish; thrust the pushpole with one hand, eat with the other. Sentry Skip. Maybe the boneys hadn't split to Cuba. Maybe Bill would gain another chance at the dickwads while they snuffled around on the bottom, a legless pack of crab-hunting hounds. Or maybe Bill didn't really give a husky.

Some folks relished time on the boat just for the experience itself. They liked to gawk as brown pelicans coasted by like pterodactyl extras in a lost world movie, to track the squawk of green parrots that whisked and chattered on urgent birdy missions. Liked to tell gross stories and offensive jokes. Belch and fart. Open closets and name skeletons. *No problema* with Skip, so long as they kept those priorities at dock time and didn't bleat, "Wish I'd caught one of those bonefish," their bottom lips wedged into doorstops, faces stricken by the tardy awareness of bounty squandered. A powerful telescope, human hindsight.

"Everything okay?" he asked when Bill returned the cellular to its pocket. Joey the phone.

"Sure. Linda wondered when I'll get in, she wants to make dinner reservations. I told her bonefish come first."

Skip grinned, lifted the graphite pushpole, pointed with the metal tip. "Some on the edge of the flat. If you're ready we can skulk up to 'em. Look right of the sailboat on the horizon, two white patches out."

"Got 'em!" Bill crowed.

As they drew closer Skip's edginess grew. His skin crawled with prickles; his tee shirt probably smelled like a sweatsock. What if another call butted into their struggle to outflank the busy, dividend bones? This was the last of the falling tide; this flat would be devoid of angling targets all too soon. He blinked up the memory of a guy he'd fished once, possibly even more cyber-bound than Bill. Guy had dialed his poolside bride every seven minutes, jittery as if he'd guzzled too much Kona Blend for breakfast. Virtual intimacy.

Maybe he should sign on for a goddam phone implant behind his ear, get it over with, Skip had thought in a rare onset of grumpiness. In the moments between kissycalls he had strained to unravel the requisite order of planetary alignments so as to conjure Guy a bonefish. But only sorcery could have rescued them from that cellular generated hell. The bane of a bonefishless day flattened a guide like roadkill, and in remembrance of that Flat Day

Skip dreaded the train looming at the end of today's tunnel. He checked the distance.

"Can you make the shot?" Skip whispered as he kicked the skiff around into position. "Any closer and they'll feel us. They're going left."

"Yeah, this is great." Bill picked up the green floating line, waved an excellent double haul and dropped the Clouser right onto their plate.

Skip quit breathing. He wished his heart wouldn't bang so loud. The boneys' lateral lines probably hummed with it. And please, he begged to a nebulous god of fish karma just in case, no phone calls. He said, "Perfect, they're coming, now bump it once. Okay! they saw it, strip it, strip it—small strips. Okay, okay, he's on it, feel for him!"

ZEEEEERRRRRRIIINNNNNNNGGGGG.

"I've got him! I've got him!" Bill shrieked, louder than his reel.

Between aortic thunders a bonefish had gummed down, knew folly, and darted for Miami. And to augment the miracle, Bill had felt the pulse of its take—that galvanic buzz as polarized lives unite by fishing line. He had tightened up quickly, and cleared his line through the rod guides.

Skip welcomed relief in a cool wash that expanded him. Piss on that phone. This fish was on! He yanged after the bonebullet with fire in his arms, kept an ear trained on Bill as he reeled backing in fast as technology goes obsolete. They gained line, but that meant the boney had knocked off, resting. Devilment in store no doubt, like a hair club weave of flyline around the nearest coral head.

Then ZEEEERRRIIINNNGGG. Another run. "Incredible!" Bill screeched. He raised his rod and pointed at the reel. Limited backing remained on the spool.

"Yeah. Worth catching all right." Skip chuckled, grateful that Bill seemed to have lost interest in his phone.

Skip grunted, shoving, bending the stiff pole, thrusting the skiff in chase. "Next time he stops, try some serious heat on him."

Bill nodded, frenzied and cranking. He pumped, then took the rod to the side. Then to the other side. Out on the flat they both spotted a flurry of bubbles. "I see him!" Bill yelled. He reeked excitement.

"Let's get him safe before some shark craves a bone-burger," Skip fretted.

Bill reeled, grunted, and panted. He pumped and leaned. The fish bolted again, and Bill rewound. Finally the bonehead came close enough to judge for size. "He's a man," Bill gasped.

"Double digits, gotta be," Skip concurred. "Careful now, they get testy at the boat."

Bill scrambled around the deck; the fish etched circuits for release. Skip climbed off the platform, leaned over the gunwale and hoisted the tired bone out of its context. One hand supported its head, one held the wrist of its tail while crystal drops sheeted off its plaided stripes of zinc and olive. Its outlined eyes rolled above its aquiline snout. "He's a beaut!" Skip's chest swelled at the touch of this Finally Bill fish, his perfect cousin of the backboned club, brave and spirited beyond its size. Little fuckers had substance. "Here, wet your hands and hold him like so, get him in the water, let him breathe."

Bill reverently took his place, cradled the muscular brine dweller while they both caught their breath. "Goddam he's strong."

Skip taped the submersed fish, grinned. "Easy ten pounder. Hold him up quick and cheese, I'll shoot." He kept his shutter finger down to record a chain of photos. Watched Bill marvel at the streamlined creature as it revived in his hands. Then he flashed on the toxic phone.

Funny, no ruckus interruptus for that whole stretch. Must have lasted fifteen minutes, though when you're working on a fish time could dissolve, compress, or dilate.

Bill glowed. "Man, this was worth the sweat."

Bill had chartered six futile days on his bonefish quest this year. Lucky he lived close enough to persist until he nailed his goal. Gave Skip time to instruct him in the physics of fly casting though, and the rewards showed. Bill had a good handle on his backcast, and his response speed had improved. Still, Skip figured that Bill might have gained the rank of bonecatcher sooner if he'd left that piece-a-shit phone in his sport utility, but said, "It's a real learning curve."

"I don't know if I learned or got lucky. He's kicking pretty strong now."

"He's ready."

Bill opened his fingers. Shook his head, awed, as the fish wagged its laser-dipped tail and dissolved in aquatic retreat. He straightened, offered his hand, laughing. "Thanks, man."

"Good job. Now the pressure's off."

"Think the next one'll be easier?"

Skip didn't. Every fish created a unique encounter; each finned through life in its own quirky style. Seasoning by bonefish slime might deliver you from a few timeworn bungles, but scale-bearers don't read the same books as hair-sprouters, and whether or not a specific fish on a given day would swallow an angler's deception—well, that's why he loved it. But before he could relate all this, Bill piped, "Wait'll Linda hears," and dug into his ample pocket.

Skip's mood lurched, then plummeted at the reappearance of the shot-blowing phone. No flats-ravaging jet skis buzzed within earshot, and day enough remained to pole

this outside edge, possibly zero in on some cruising singles. They tended to be the larger bones, Width to them.
Yeah. He sighed. At least that gap in the incessant clangor
had allowed Bill to touch his first bonefish.

"Damn," Bill muttered. He fiddled with the phone.
Slapped it a time or two. Popped open the battery compartment. "Damn," he repeated. "Looks like the battery's
dead."

Skip grinned. Elation reigned. "*No problema*. I know
the address of Bonefish Central."

SIX

Bonefish Heaven

Air 82 degrees, water 80, late February, Florida Keys. Bright winter sun toasts the day. Lime blossoms and Hong Kong orchid trees scent the southeast wind, while mud puffs and tail flashes cover the flats. Bonefish. Whole schools of them form fish-shaped twinkles in green brine as clear as air. They cruise like Spring Breakers, reveling in the warmth.

"We're trapped!" Skip's whisper strains to reach the bow of the skiff. He wants to shout, laugh, yell. But he says, "Don't move!"

His client, Malcolm, stiffens, nods, the dark bill of his cap making a crisp up-down. Skip can see him hold his breath, and he, too, is afraid to blink or turn his head. Hordes of bonefish surround them. "Try a cast at the ones on the left, just flip it out, easy, easy."

Many anglers bumble the short, quick casts, so Skip's confidence in the outcome stalls. Maybe muscle memory takes over, or maybe they envision a majestic television cast, and boom, out slings a big goober. Consequently, their fly plops miles beyond hungry bonefish lips. Lines them. Or the motion alarms the skittish fish and they wink out of sight in a flurry of bonedust. But bless this guy with nerves of steel, he barely flicks his rod tip and releases the line. The Clouser minnow slips into the water near, but not too near, the approaching bones. Skip risks a breath. "Perfect, perfect, let it sit. Wait, wait. Okay, jump it once, okay, okay."

This trip came just in time. Yesterday had been—Real.

Skip's blood had started boiling well before 7:00 A.M. Please, he cursed, let there be a Special Place in Hell reserved for mannerless twits who park at the gas pump of a quik mart and then wander in to do their weekly grocery shopping. There they stood, dawdling inside, flapping their ill-bred yaps (probably swapping false memory fables of childhood abuse), way too vapid to see that five other cars had by now congealed around their rusted junker. In resentful adherence to social constraints Skip bid them swift arrival to that Special Place.

He ended up having to park with the boat trailer askew. The cockeyed angle of the gas hose kept the nozzle from shutting off properly, so when he removed it from the boat's filler tube, High Octane splashed down along one side of the deck. Perfect. Aaah, the heady bouquet of unleaded in the morning. He had dashed home, washed, dried, waxed, and buffed the deck. All before starting his day's work. His temples throbbed.

His two clients that day turned out to be big, friendly guys who brightened his mood by alleging that they could fish. At least his mood stayed sunny for a while, until rather ho-hum bonefish sightings began to strike it down. Oh, they had a decent number of shots at fish, a few cruisers, scattered ones and twos tailing. Enough, anyway, for a seasoned saltwater angler. But way too few for rookies, who, of course, have to learn by doing and just naturally scare more fish than they catch. By the end of their first day most rookies generally start to click, but if that is their only day to fish, well, as Grandpa said all the time, Hell's Bells.

So anyway, Skip would have killed (preferably a quik mart grocery shopper) for a house mud. That's what flats guides call it when the bonefish jam together, snarfling and digging up the bottom in deeper water, creating muds of a residential size. Hard to miss them, so even the most flats blind fisherman gets the chance to throw. These guys, though, could see the fish, and could actually cast fairly well, but their technique clashed with the conditions: very light wind, which demands extreme finesse. They had fastened onto that more brawny, splashy method that you often see cold country, fresh water fishermen use. It was tough, over the course of just one day, to adjust their style. And so they all had to laugh, often.

ZING, the spinning rod would scream through the air as the bigger one, Clete, who looked like a football player, launched another shrimp into orbit.

Skip imagined snickers among the small pods of bonefish. Why bite shrimp on the hook when you could wait for a big guy to fling one your way?

"Not so hard," he cautioned Clete, thinking perhaps NASA should be alerted to these new hazards in space.

"Sure." ZING.

"Not so Hard," Skip repeated, repeatedly.

SNAPPPP! went the spinning rod, in response to a Bassmaster style hookset.

"Woops!" said Clete.

Shattered rod aside, they each boated a mix of toothy by catch—barracuda, small lemon sharks, even a reticulated trunkfish—considering their technique, a stunning accomplishment. The target species, however, remained aloof. So Skip went looking for the last dumb bonefish in Monroe County, or at least one consumed with gluttony, and finally found him at Mud Cottage.

"About six, six and a half," he extolled, scooping the disgruntled boney from the water. Droplets sparkled off its fins like sunlight on quartz. While Don and Clete thumped each other on the back, Skip glanced around for that star to rise in the East. Happy for Don? Say thrilled, and so relieved he almost hurled his lunch. The struggle of mentally *willing* him to hook a bonefish, all while trying to provide the Best Day Fishing of His Life, had just about sucked him dry.

Then comes a trip like today, with a fly-fisher like nerves-of-steel Malcolm. The guy proves that sometimes a blessing arrives in client's clothing—a day with him on the boat feels as restorative as a vacation.

"Long strip, long strip, wait." Skip's peripheral vision scopes another band of bonefish—plowing the bottom, too lost in arthropod pursuit to sense the tension of their fellow vertebrates nearby. He hopes they decide to stick around. Cue the laugh track.

Mal is a miracle man, a gift. Skip wishes that some method existed to pop a mold off him like a prototype boat. Then he could sell the copies to guides everywhere: The Perfect Client. They could unwrap him, take him fishing every time they felt terminally bummed and needed a lift. Mal doesn't just hear—he Listens. Does exactly what Skip says, and exactly when. Although not a strong caster, around forty feet on average, his ability to stay out of his own way has served him well. And there are few things more wonderful to a guide when he puts his client on a fish, than for the client to simply go ahead and catch it.

Skip continues coaching Mal's retrieve. "Now, short strip, short strip, eat it fish! Eat it! All right!"

The bonefish garbages the fly.

"I saw him eat!" Mal's voice wobbles, choked with thrill.

"Clear your line," Skip intones, trying to exude calm so Mal won't get jittery and forget everything, including his own name. Hooking up to a good fish could still tangle Skip's tongue. Inside a balloon replaces his stomach and his heart rapid-fires.

Mal lifts his eight-weight, sticks it out. His Supplex-bundled frame quivers with awkward grace and his fly-line slicks through rod guides like pouring oil. Oh, the beauty of line control.

Life is good. Skip feels high enough to float. If Mal's line avoids the Gordian cliché, if the boney doesn't scrape against a coral head . . . Mal's reel sings out its version of "Bonefish Number Five," yes, his fifth fish of the day, and Skip poles, poles, poles his way to fitness.

Some time before their subjective Easter Mal manages to get most of his fly line back on the reel. "Here he is, here he is!" he squeaks, his voice breaking as he hops around on the casting deck. He beams with joy.

"Oh, man, oh, man," Skip babbles, scampering to help him boat and release the precious bone. One of the fine green ones, with a deep olive back and shimmery slate side stripes. Mal murmurs as Skip hefts the fish, pumping it out of the water to gauge its weight. "Chunky. Want to hold him?"

Mal chuckles like a flock of happy Mallards. He wets his hands, eager, and gapes at the slime-slick, grass-scented, shrimp-breathed fish like a new dad. Skip quickly tapes the bonefish, pointy snout to blued fork. "Thirty-one inches! You've outdone yourself!"

He steps back and watches them, Mal bent over the gunwale, his face painted with delight, the bonefish relaxing in the water, no panic. At times Skip believes these fish somehow understand they'll be released, decoding it in some moist piscine, lateral line way. Or maybe this was one of the more highly educated Keys bonefish, seen armies of Crazy Charlies and Clousers, legions of guides and anglers, been hooked a time or three. Hard to fool. Even more of a coup.

Days like this yield a saltier sea breeze, a softer sun glare. Instead of angelic choirs and clouds pouring golden rays, Skip hears an osprey's whistle, sees Mal's radiant face. May not be Bonefish Heaven, but it will do.

SEVEN

 *Sunset Drag*

Drift a skiff on the tide flow between Florida Bay and Hawk Channel, and from gusty springtime into muggy summer you'll float over tarpon big enough (and likely old enough) to vote. They course the deep blue channels under the Overseas Highway bridges from one side of the Keys to the other, through water like windows.

On these currents wafted a certain fishing guide well-known to Skip as John, the guy you can send spin fishermen to during tarpon season—Skip liked to stick with sight casting and for tarpon, that meant fly. John and his client had plugged away under the bridge known as Channel Five since, to the guide's sense of time, roughly the Mesozoic era. A brisk wind lifted whitecaps from the depths and salted the humidity, while cormorants splayed creosote wings out to dry and honked their greedy noises from every handy perch.

Like most guides during that slice of the year, John recalled fatigue with a wistful smile, relative to his current state. Tired? Shot through with exhaustion might convey it better. His energy level resembled Swiss cheese. He had fished a boatload of live bait for tarpon trips under the bridges this season, which often demands a unique schedule. At times the tarpon bite pinfish, or whatever bait *du jour*, most aggressively before the farm report and after the nightly news, so you might have to schedule such a tarpon trip from 3:00 A.M. to 9:00 A.M., and another voyage may last from 6:00 P.M. until midnight. And of course as many days as possible in between you tried to sandwich in those sunburn special fishing adventures. Most of the Keys guides sock away the bulk of their year's income during the tarpon migration, so only a small minority feels willing to pass up a charter. The sleep deprivation and the incessant hammering of the sun, wind, and waves taxes even the hardiest salt, though, and frazzled becomes the cast of the season. Tempers ignite. Rods break. Minds warp. Imagine feeling so whipped that you dream about sleeping. And that's only the first month.

Tired John's client had launched a one-day career of missing hook sets and quickly breaking off the rest of several eager and cooperative tarpon that had done their best to entertain. All around them, all day, tarpon had porpoised lazily, swam in daisy chains of bronzed indigo dorsal against turquoise sea, or rocketed skyward on the ends of other fishermen's lines like so many silver-suited acrobats.

Then a lull had spread under the bridge. Fish quit rolling. Guides fired up their outboards, rumbled toward their docks and their rewards. The light softened to gold, the lemon sun slid toward the Gulf of Mexico. Chances for a catch before this trip expired had entered the dubious zone. Tired John felt hot, sick, sweaty, and about ready to stuff the fishing guide bidness. Go sell ladies' shoes, or at least go get in the air conditioning and cloud his judgement with a series of adult beverages.

Out of the blue Tired John spotted the arched verdigris back of the last cheerful, rolling fish this side of Belize.

"There, there," he called, to point out to Career this snowball's hope at catching a tarpon today. He prayed the guy still had some substance on his hook that resembled fish food and that it hadn't tangled into a weedburger. And that when, or if, the tarpon garbaged the bait the guy wouldn't jerk it out of his maw. Or forget to bow—give slack—when the tarpon jumped. He hoped just this once that Career would do his job.

Give an angler the option of picking between luck and skill, as if some genie might bestow either attribute upon him, and often luck will prove the more frequent choice. And so it came to pass that in that tired and sunset moment, luck prevailed.

The tarpon glommed. And, in a fury, rose to face the wielder of the sharpness. Insult had been added to interruption of its happy afternoon glide. Chrome. Flashbulb. Foam.

"Hit him! Hit him! Like you mean it!" screeched Tired John.

And so Career hooked up. Remembered to bow. Everything. But forty-five shakes later it did not look as if Career would best the outraged fish. The Tea Time tarpon had obviously chowed down on power sea biscuits along with its crab chowder. In an effort to rid itself of its attachment to that pesky standing creature, or perhaps merely to seek respite and pout, it had set sail for the Marquesas. Tired John idled the skiff along behind. A long.

Swear words began to form patterns in Tired John's mind, began to spill out his mouth. It sucked major dog sniff to make a tarpon overtired; you don't want to damage the key to your livelihood. And the sky had turned real picturesque. Streams of grenadine and pineapple spilled from under clouds gone cyanotic. That meant Late. And those colors brought to mind the more pleasant aspects of judgement clouding that he had decided to pursue for the evening. Resolute, Tired John shifted the outboard motor into neutral. Walked to the bow of the skiff. Career continued his grunting, reeling, and pumping exercises—no more gym workouts needed for him this week. Tired John reached down to Career's reel and tightened the drag screw, all the way home.

Career looked by his thumb, alarmed. "What are you doing?"

"It's time to go," Tired John replied. "Now get him in or break him off." Expletives deleted.

But as so often happens when fishing, the planned event disintegrated. Almost as if it had sensed the change in current on the line, the change in tension among those strange pink uprights, Tea Time blew up. Climbed the sky and left the state.

Yanked by the sudden jolt from this large-scaled hurricane, the reel twisted free of the reel seat. The rapidly disappearing fish jerked the reel straight out along the rod and right through the rod guides—and stripped the rod bare. All over in a snap.

Now Tired John had only bought that particular fishing rod a couple days prior to the foray with Career, so during his next non-working hour of unclouded judgement he drove back to the rod builder's shop. He had thought maybe he would tell the guy that it had fallen apart (not exactly) while fighting this humongous tarpon (true) and maybe the guy would fix it for free (not likely), or at least charge him no more for repairs than he had earned on that ill-fated charter (sure). He handed the mangled, guide-less stick to its creator.

"What the hell happened here?" the rod wrapper gasped.

"Oh, that." All the excuses stuck in Tired John's throat, and instead out came, "Uh, well, my client hooked up five minutes before quitting time and he wouldn't put enough heat on the fish so I had to crank the reel down into Sunset Drag."

EIGHT

Bone Fever

One more minute reeling and my arms will seize. They probably look like Popeye's right now. Real attractive. And this heat is giving me a sweat hemorrhage. Behind me nice old Capt. Jessup clears his throat.

"Try pulling up on his head when he gets close to the boat, Sharon," I tell the struggling lady angler.

My fly rod quivers in its arc. I straighten my back, gulp hot sweet air. "It's objecting to that." Who'd think a bone-fish had so much fight? Who'd think I'd ever hook one? Not the former dear Chad, rhymes with cad. But here I am. On a flats skiff in the Florida Keys, complete with a salty guide to urge me on. The sunbaked skin on his hands looks like an elephant's, if elephants came in mahogany. He has that same huge patience, too.

And has he ever shown it—all day, right from first light when I stumbled to the dock feeling like a bad case of burnout. He probably took one look and wished he'd stayed home—me with novice smeared all over my face like a kid caught licking frosting. But I'd booked this bonefish trip as a birthday gift for Chad. Before. He sure wouldn't get presents from me now, and I couldn't let it go to waste.

The lady, girl really, falters a little. Looks tired. Looked weary this morning, eyes burned in deep as if sleep were a stranger. I encourage her some, "When you rest, the fish rests. Makes the fight take longer." I know tired when I see it. After forty years of fishing the flats it's an old friend. Strange life, pushing a boat around while people throw strings and feathers at fish. Days so long you forget your name, forget if an event happened today or yesterday. No part of the Fortune 500, but that's no big deal. Got that blue and green water shifting, golden sunlight on pink spoonbill wings. . . . "Get you a rhythm going now." She needs reminding. Way the sun's burnt a hole in the sky and not but a whiff of wind, it's a wonder she's held up this long. Got smooth hands and hesitant feet. "Pump and reel."

"I'm pumped dry," I grunt, but I don't quit. Not since that lucky cast—how long ago?—to a group, pod Capt. Jessup says, of tailing bonefish. Their busy fins had cut the surface glaze like miniature swords. Diamonds twinkled off their tails and I had watched, enchanted, lost in irrelevant thoughts of childhood fairy tales, prismatic wonderlands and silly little fish doing headstands. Until Capt. Jessup prompted me to try a cast and for once I did something right, even if by accident. Since then this feels-like-a-whale bonefish and I have shared our lives. I feel connected to it, in an unbalanced but dynamic way, by more than a 9-weight flyline. We both want to survive, somehow. Despite the gap in our perspectives, it seems like my first honest relationship in ages. At least this one is based on more than empty letters forming empty words. I've missed substance.

Dad would have loved this trip. He used to fly-fish little rocky creeks with me, me elbow high and tangled all the time, him pointing out the rich greens, reds, and golds on the brookies. Talk about patience. If he were still here I could have given the trip to him, stayed home and hidden my shame. Played an actress of depression. But no. Instead I hunt for the leftover crumbs of joy hidden in those time-crusted memories. As if the balm of fly casting, or this tropical scenery, could heal my broken parts. Meanwhile my mayonnaise skin turns the color of new lipstick, my feet burn, my knees shake, and my forearms feel like balloons. How do people ever land hundred pound tarpon? This old bonefish really has spirit; would I fight this hard for myself? "It feels like it's holding on to the bottom."

I call to the girl from the poling platform, "Are you gaining any line? Need me to pole after him some?" Can't see her fly reel there in front of her. Nothing but backing shows out the rod tip. It'd be good if she could pump him in some so I wouldn't have to hump this skiff after him. Even with no wind today these achy bones have taken to liking work less and less. Boat gets heavier every year. Should quit this business, get a job less physical, old fart like me. Way out on the blue-green flat the bonefish comes up, turns. "There he is, three o'clock!" My pulse thunders at the sight. That fish'll go over twelve pounds. Helluva fish. "He's a big one! A whale!"

A flash like chrome glints in the sun, then a broad dark back, then my reel screams loud as a ravenous seagull. My bonefish takes off on another run. It moves faster than any other fish I've seen, any other *thing* I've seen, shoving the water with the force of a hyperactive snowplow. "Did you see that?" Then I shriek, "What do I do now?" My empty mind glitters from the sunlight reflected off this water, clear as tears. Just before this trip I invested in a weekend at a saltwater fly-fishing school, adding to never mastered skills, but all knowledge has faded under this scorching sky and the pressure of a real bonefish about to spool me.

"Get ready to reel in fast, I'm going after him." I lean hard into the graphite pushpole, shove the skiff after the bulge of water heading for Cuba. A reel-smoker. My eyes burn to look at him, to admire the width of his shoulders. "You're doing good, this is some hot fish." Strong for this time of year, still muggy and all. Water's cooled some from the bath water of summer but he's fighting like a January bone. And Sharon, gritting her teeth like her life depended on this. Didn't seem that way at first, head kind of low and a soft pain in her smoky eyes. Proves a good bonefish can bring out the heart in a person, show what they're made of.

Capt. Jessup acts like I can do this, like it's expected, people do it every day, big old honking bonefish pulling on their lines. Wish I had that same confidence. When Chad left, the street lamp shine off the pale head in the passenger seat said it all. Loser. But I reel hard and squint into the glare. "I see the fly line! I'm gaining on it!" A shiver of hope thrills up my sore back. I never knew it took back muscles to fish; this is a real workout. Even my legs hurt. My lungs huff in air that tastes like hot perfume. I won't smell like perfume by the time I get this bonefish to the boat, skiff. If I get it. But I can't quit. After the kind words and glances of pity at work, this trip's a comfort. It sure beats raking leaves in front of an empty house in a town shrunk too small overnight. The fly line shudders, tremors echo to my hand from the bonefish shaking its head out there in the water. Probably looking for a piece of seaweed, sargassum Capt. Jessup calls it, to wrap the line around, break me off. No, no way, bonefish. I reel furiously, muscles past burning.

Cramping. I need this fish. I beg. Oh please come on, please I'm so tired. Something in my head pops, like how ears do in an airplane, but a bigger sensation, and more clear. I smell briny air and warm wood and flowers. I hear the cavernous rumble of Capt. Jessup's chuckle in the background, the squeak of a white tern circling overhead in a sky that radiates a hard blue beauty. My limbs weigh less, and the world sparkles, as if I'd stepped out of a dark room through a screen door into light.

"Here he comes!" I stake the skiff, scramble down from the poling platform to help Sharon. Funny how aches and pains disappear when a big bonefish comes in. Good to see that spark in the girl as she turns around. Got that huntress look, connected to the fish by a million years of instinct and that's all that's real to her right now.

Capt. Jessup reaches over the side of the skiff and waits. I reel and bend and twist, trying to get this silver log is what it seems like now, close enough for him to grab. I'm panting, sweating, babbling. "Oh, look at it! Look at those little diamonds on its back!" I thought these fish were all silver, or gray, but no. It has an intricate geometric pattern, olive chevrons blending into stripes somehow, like an M.C. Escher print, but animate. Capt. Jessup holds it in the water and I get my camera. I hope the luminous blue that edges its fins will show up on film; they look dipped in laser paint. And what a funny rubbery mouth. The fish looks at me taking its picture—what must it feel? It has big ringed eyes and I cradle it now and it smells like seafoam as it rests in the water, catching its breath. Its body is hard, all muscle and bone and will to survive, but somehow almost trusting me to hold it a while until it's ready, not wiggling. My heart slows back down and my throat is scratchy and dry. I hear the whine of the motor drive on the camera as Capt. Jessup takes some shots of us. Me and my bonefish. I want to hold this fish forever, stay in thrall to the moment, just me and Capt. Jessup and my long, fat, wide, lovely first bonefish. "It's beautiful! I can't believe I did it. I really did it!"

"Yes ma'am. You fought him good. He must be every bit of twelve pounds, this one. Not your everyday bonefish and that's a fact." Sharon looks whipped but her face glows. She's kind of a pretty girl when she's not so glum. That bonefish tuned her right up. Worth seeing, makes a good day golden. "If you get some decent prints from this roll of film, I'd really like one of you and that big guy there. Wife Ellen collects 'em, pictures of the best fish and best days on the water. She puts 'em in albums."

The bonefish, my bonefish, pushes against my fingers, starting to kick, ready to swim away. Away from a bizarre experience—eating a meal that bites back, then held by pink things without scales. "Have a nice life, guy," I say when it wriggles free from my hands. It slips through the water, blending in, disappearing. Alive. It leaves me behind, calm from exhaustion, clearheaded for the first time in weeks. Grateful.

"Of course I'll send you pictures, Capt. Jessup. I couldn't have done it without you. I'll never forget this day. Never. Thank you." My mind feels cool, minty, as if my brain had brushed its teeth, rinsing away my tangled sense of illusion along with my tortured thoughts of what's-his-name. Leaving behind all that's clean and real, and alive. I picture stacks of photo albums full of smiling faces and glossy fish, wonder if the others felt changed. "What a great way to make a living, doing this for people. It's really wonderful!"

I check the hook on Sharon's fly, give it a couple strokes with the file to sharpen it up again. I can't help but smile. "Just need a strong back and a weak mind, ma'am. No big deal."

NINE

Will Work for Permit

"Might get shots at permit." Skip smiled into the phone, emphasized the might.

A new client dangled in the ether, clutching his Minnesota receiver in a place where snow had drifted into meringue castles. Guy's thumbs probably had blisters from paging through slick fishing monthlies, his beliefs anchored in TV productions where four days compress into thirty enchanted minutes. Visions of flats like opal windows, tropical balm, and exalted fish had combined to jar his terminal winter blahs. Or so Skip thought.

"Great, see you Wednesday the thirteenth." Morbid dread of another blast of winter fills up the bookings calendar.

March in the Florida Keys. Wind, warmth, permit. Ought to have greeting cards with goofy verses for the occasion, make it a regional event, hear an unctuous announcer during station breaks—"Celebrate Florida Permit Month. Book Early." Always here, along with the usual abundance of bonefish, they just clicked better in some seasons than in others. Yeah. Like the Fall months. Get that water temperature just so on the flats and here they'd come.

"Isn't it usually permit who get shots at you?" his wife, Shelly, giggled. She clicked the pause button on the VCR to restart the movie.

Skip grinned. "Usually."

Little bastids would prowl behind your skiff while you poled the flats searching for bonefish. They would eagerly munch on tiny shrimp and crabs that floated free in the mud puffs made by the tip of your pushpole. When you finally sensed Something Watching You and squinted into the glaze, there they laughed. As if to say "Hi, catching any?" Then they would angle their smooth reflective sides a micron to vanish like spooks while you stared. Shape shifting fish. Smoked mirrors.

Wednesday's guy was full of woe.

Early sun beamed into the spice of jacaranda wind as he lowered himself from dock to skiff, as stiffly as a man who suffered from terminal impaction. A grimace dulled his features.

Skip wondered what sort of karmic whiplash had clobbered this otherwise apparently healthy dude. Maybe his pet fly rod exploded.

One of Skip's favorite rods had blown up on a big fish a little while back, and its loss had sure smarted until its replacement arrived. Normally though, for a guy this age the biggies were money or women. "Chad, you feel okay?"

Chad nodded, wavered a grin. His eyes drooped. "Lately, life sucks."

"Today excepted." Skip countered with a flash of positive face Number Ten. Most of his clients arrived so jazzed that he had a hard time matching their enthusiasm, but

Chad needed a cheerleader. He slumped onto the cushion, his surface about to rust from that injured essence of a chronic loser. A little encouragement might get him venting, though, offer some relief. Just another facet in the job description—hell, Skip figured guides hear as many confessions as priests and bartenders.

Chad sighed, stared from his mental Canada while Skip stowed his duffel, looped his new 8- and 10-weight fly rods into the racks, plopped his deli rye and designer water into the cooler. Looked like you could scratch off bucks as the cause of this guy's problem.

"Lucky we've got some wind." Skip cranked the outboard, untied the dock lines. "Takes permit fishing from impossible to just unlikely."

Chad brightened a shade. His vibes embodied what happens when you wind monofilament too tight on a cheap reel—it stores so much energy that it squeezes the reel apart. Sighting the cutlass fin of a permit would shake him loose. Those fish reflected more than sunlight or sand bottom; they transmitted clarity from here into memory.

The skiff curved across a shallow dish of brine with clouds piled above the rim—whipped cream on a lime pie. Skip's stomach growled. "Okay now, feed out some line, get ready." They had reached the rocky edge of a rippled flat.

Chad peeled off fly line, whooshed his 10-weight. The Merkin crashed into the water twenty feet out.

Uh oh. It'd be a compliment to call him a poor caster, Skip thought. He wondered, often, whether it was ignorance or arrogance when people decided to fly-fish for a species before acquiring the skills. Maybe they just forget *those* paragraphs in the glossies. "New rod?"

"Yeah, it's the gnat's ass. But I usually throw my old seven, so I can't quite, um. . . . " Gloom took over.

Skip staked the boat, hopped from the poling platform, cheerily offering, "Maybe I can help your distance. You double haul?" Obviously, you could scratch off the death of his favorite fly rod, too. That left the worst one. Poor sucker.

Chad made sounds of relief and confusion. "No-o-o. On our trout streams and little lakes, um, I haven't really needed to. . . ."

They spent some time on casting practice. Chad went through the obligatory spell when he lost all motor skills, wrapped himself, and Skip, in fly line necklaces, stepped inside his coils, and invented some fresh epithets.

Skip called a break, chugged down a long slug of orange liquid to replace electrolytes, and passed Chad his yuppie water. "I think you're getting it." Athletic and coordinated, Chad probably ruled on his home rivers, but without mastering the double haul for saltwater, on the flats he'd be toast. Without the caviar.

He lit up at Skip's compliment. "Really?"

"You're quick. Gotta do it until every motion turns to reflex, though, until it jells into habit, develop muscle memory," Skip warned. Not enough folks he taught would follow through. They returned to work in Otherwhere, strove upwardly to whatever avail, and never practiced those moves again until they stepped onto their unsuspecting guide's boat the next year. Fully unrehearsed. Way Skip figured, life was fatal—learn to cast. "Let's try it. Remember, focus, but try to stay loose."

Chad shrugged, wobbled his neck like he'd just sensed his balance, wired between tired and tense. Strung tight and hanging. "I'm ready."

Skip poled west across the flat and checked the range of his doubts. It took resolve to face a permit, a muse of a fish that deftly employed its radar shields to conceal itself. But if fishing were predictable, who would go? A fresh scent drifted in, wet seagrass and salt sweetness; something warm tickled his brain. Two distant purple jet skis chain-sawed through decorum. Overhead an osprey floated in suspense and a racket of monk parakeets flapped above the mangroves. He jerked his head around to surprise the tricks of refraction before they arose. Like trying to sneak up on your childhood.

"There!" Skip choked, shoved the stern so Chad could glimpse the luster. "Throw at 'em! Four o'clock, point your rod, yes, yes, throw, now, hurry!" A little stoked, yeah.

Chad threw. Skip ducked. The permit dialed down their rheostats and vanished.

"Did you see 'em, did you see 'em?"

Chad's mouth hung open. He lifted his jaw. "They're like holograms."

"Yeah," Skip hummed, proud of the little bastids. Invented morphing. "High tech."

"Do you think we'll get another shot at them?" Interest sparkled all over him.

Will I win the lottery? Will we contact extraterrestrials —other than these? Skip the Oracle poled on, tried to answer the unknown. "With them, probably not, they've seen us and had their jollies. Maybe others. Sometimes they even nap here." He began to build a measure of hope for old Chad. At least he wasn't some tar foot who moved around on the boat too much, or sat on the downwind side, making it tip more and wave slap louder. And that one flash of permit radiance had wiped considerable stain off his spirit. Squeezed a shine out of him. Maybe he could sprout an interest in life yet.

"Naps? Fish?"

"Sure. More so on calmer days. They float near the surface, shimmer in the sunlight, pointy black dorsals sticking out, man. . . ."

Chad looked wistful.

Skip continued, describing how he had ruined dinner over permit once. "I'd fished late trying to find 'em for my angler. Guy had jonesed for 'em all day and I came home pushpole whipped, sun dried, and full of permit afterglow. So tired that I couldn't remember if I'd done some things that day or the day before. My wife, Shelly, had planned a cookout, though, so I hurried through the boat cleaning stuff, and while she tossed the salad I juggled phone calls and watched the chicken on the grill. Well, sorta. As we sawed through the blackened crusts at the table I felt a little guilty for my lack of vigilance. So I go, "Hey, how about these Cinder Vittles?" She showed her teeth like a barracuda. Not all that amused. Then I said to her, "My guy hooked a twenty pound permit." Her ears perked up, and so then we got to jabbering on about how totally cool they are and all, it made the burnt chicken history. I'm just glad the little bastids swim and don't walk, if you know what I mean. Shelly really loves 'em."

Chad chuckled. "Yeah, think I know what you mean." Then his light sucked into a hole of quiet, a profile of logo cap against blinding sparkles, reflecting off water like green glass. "I had a wife."

Uh oh. Skip heard the Had, didn't need the rest of the page. Like he had a choice. *Damn, where's a fish when you need one? Worse than cops.* He scanned the ripples as if focus and forceful eyes could manifest one. "Hey, throw at that trunkfish. They're good practice. Poor man's permit."

Chad tossed the fly, reached back, pushed forward, repeated, let go. Plop. Same latitude. He really was getting it.

"Hey, good cast, good cast. Little strips now."

The trunkfish lit up, pale blue spots iridescing against its cocoa body as it scootered about in the water. Shelly adored their silly pectorals that flapped like wings, and their tiny mouths, so hard to hook.

Chad gasped, his reel screeched, and Skip cheered while the trunkfish scurried for safety. "They pull pretty hard, don't they?"

"I didn't feel him take it," he started, then, "Woops! He's off."

"They come unbuttoned easy."

He reeled in. "I tried to relax, like you said."

"It shows."

"She fished down here last fall."

Damn. "Yeah? Catch some fish?"

"Don't know. Been afraid to call her. Made an ass of myself."

Skip blew exhaust, glanced up. The sky held blue an absolute value much lighter than Chad's. He'd seen shame fairly cripple people. The permutations of asinine behavior that we *homo*-not-so-*sapiens* can arrange for ourselves exercised every meaning of awful. Take that long ride down Infernal Road. Or covet the grass in another's pasture. Hell, safety and character issues aside, nowadays you couldn't even assume that it was actually grass. Like Grandma always said, "More than one way to make a horse's hangdown of yourself." "Now you're casting better, let's talk line control."

He turned, forehead crinkled. "Okay. What?"

"When the fly hits the water, pull once hard, stripping it behind you into the deck of the boat. Gets the slack out, and usually the rest of the line follows as you strip it on in. Then when you hook up there's less chance of birds nest soup popping off your rod guides."

"Cool. I'll try."

For a March day it scored pretty damn decent. Forget kite-flying. Wind salted the air at an unusual twelve knots, and a dandelion sun warmed them without melting their flesh like wax. Skip tacked, taking an oblique angle across the brown-green flat. On a bonefish hunt, but mindful of the quest for those cheeky permit.

Chad swiveled, "You ever do church?"

No one had ever asked him that, out fishing. "Not exactly. I fly-fish for permit—figure that it's about the same."

"Mothers." He rubbed his face. "Said I'd feel better, just trying to help, I guess. But I can't get into it. Same how?"

Skip had to grin. "Blind faith, belief in supernatural beings. You stand on a raised platform and make sacrifices—of flies and hope, in this case. Feel rapture now and then. Nice sanctuary, too."

Chad smiled, held it, then turned back and scanned the shallows. "What's that?"

"Barracuda. Try him."

He fired one out but the barracuda shrugged it off. He practiced stripping in his line.

"Bonefish mud, see it?" A chalky plume streaked the salt.

He pointed with his rod tip until Skip said, "There. Wait, I'll get you closer."

Chad lifted the eight-weight, leaned the ten against the console, eased himself back onto the casting platform. He searched for the mud bloom, pointed, "There?"

"Yeah. Wait. Wait. Now."

He false cast too many times, finally released. Off to the left. Skip fidgeted, reminded himself to tell Chad to chill the false casts. Too much motion warns the fish. "Pick it up, throw again, one move." He lifted, hauled, sailed one into the general zone. "Good, get your slack. Strip it."

"I feel it!" He squeaked as the line came tight.

"Clear your line! Your feet!" Snap. Too late.

Chad looked down at his left deck shoe, on the fly line. "Oh, man. . . ."

"Everyone's done it at least once. Let's get ready again. Day's not over."

They took a break, tied another Clouser minnow on the leader of the eight-weight, chewed up their sandwiches, watered their inner cells. Skip checked his watch. Good tide. "Showtime."

Chad repaired to the casting deck, wiggled his neck, huffed, shook out his fingers. "I thought I was in decent shape, but I'm getting stiff."

"People don't stay outside like they used to. Strength indoors isn't like endurance out here."

"I hear ya."

"Got your ten ready?"

"You see something?"

"Between us and that little cay, couple hundred yards, point, left, left, there." Skip knew better than to pin his hopes on the wrong donkey, like getting old Chad a permit. But if he did, maybe that overflow of joy would surf him over the blockage he'd installed in himself.

"Those glints are fish?"

"Hold on until we're closer. And make this cast a dick-saver."

Skip stroked the skiff toward the tailing permit, the sheen of saltwater now diamonds on their sharply curved dorsals of pewter and onyx. Their moonglow bodies flickered like a trace of ideas. A hoped-for wish.

Skip didn't remember when he quit breathing, but his chest seized tight from poling without oxygen. In guide time, right then, permit meant air. Living sea quartz who contain inspiration, completion, in their glass bodies.

"Whoooaaa," Chad muttered.

"Sink or swim," Skip whispered.

In dream style frames the background went mute. No dive boats puttered by, sprouting wet-suited, wet-headed vacationers out for their nitrogen gamble. No Miami to Cancun jets foam-lined the sky. Skip's nostrils flared with sea soup and fish slime, the planetary fluid. His vision tunneled, seeing only the liquid flash of turquoise, crystal, moonstone, jet.

Chad grunted. Toss, back, push; haul, back, Punch! The Merkin sailed, arced, settled.

Skip heaved for breath. "Your slack! Yes! Move it in front of them! Let it sink! He's looking, feed him! FEED him!" He pretzeled with body language, unseen. He twisted, urgency vital, to sway the fish, to BITE an imitation of life.

"Unnhnnh." Chad bled sounds. His body bent like a longbow, his fly rod the arrow, he zeroed on the goal. Life, not death, the crux.

"Tighten your slack!" Sweat ran down Skip's back. His throat ached.

"Uhhnnhh." Screeeeee. "Aaaahhhhh! He's! I! Aaahhh!" Fly line snaked off the deck. Chad whipped his eyes to his feet. Clear.

The Impossible veered, wavered, gave way. The atmosphere crackled back into its wider reality. Terns squabbled, waves splashed. And an indignant sphere fizzed toward another galaxy like a longhaired star.

Skip soared. He pushed the skiff toward honor, his very blood laughing.

Chad held on.

Potentialities boiled: knots could part, lines snap, hooks pull. In this context, real time emptied itself. In guide time, stretched like Elastic Man by worry, the permit skimmed to hand right before Skip's subjective Christmas. It browned its fins into brackets of anger. Buttercup flanks and black eyes, Jersey cow soft, splashed contrast and depth against skin carved from moonbeams.

Chad couldn't talk. Skip didn't bother. Not now. Skip hugged the prize and handed him to Chad, whose arms shook with treasure all the way into the sea. This would be hard to top as an omen for change of luck. Skip could almost swear that he heard the microprocessors whir as Chad shivered, evaluated, understood. When an angler meets tangible magic, when he touches an evasive permit, it matters. Holds swing. He wiped his face with a sleeve, felt big and small at once. Thought he saw a phone call in Chad's future. Allure inside this oracle joke, after all.

TEN

Just the Tip of the Bonefish

Coffee slopped from his mug as Skip dashed to the phone. He dodged two strung fly rods leaning against the wall, noticed that their tips had scratched marks like pencil scribbles. He flicked his eyes to the clock on the stove. 6:12. Ante meridian.

"Hey! It's glass slick!" The familiar voice rasped thick with morning gravel. One of his sunburned-brain buds, another fishing guide, sounded sleepy but ready to head out early. When the water mirrored off he liked to streak deep through the illusion of floating Keys into Florida Bay after baby tarpon, loved to fish those tannic waters along the Everglades shorelines. Hell of a long run, though.

"I know." Skip smiled. They often traded scuttlebutt on fishing spots—who allegedly caught what, and where. But he didn't need backcountry news today. "I'll be out front, looking for bones." Meaning he planned to work the diamond clear waters on the ocean side of the Keys.

Light spilled from his kitchen window into the back-yard, where plumeria blooms suspended in darkness quiet as butterfly wings. Dawn promised one of those legendary mornings that made Skip's skin want to burst. The bonefish would poke their tails out of those shiny salt-soup flats like metal sculptures in pools of mercury. He loved summer. Yeah. He wondered if his client today numbered among the casting impaired.

He did.

Skip poled his skiff toward a patch of tailing bonefish. They seemed happy, grubbing crustaceans for breakfast, their fins looking like sharpened blades as they twinkled and sliced between mangrove shoots. "Okay Ken, get ready," he stage whispered to his client. A belted kingfisher chuckled in answer, scolding at their intrusion.

Ken quickly lifted his fly line from where it had drooled beside the skiff and flicked away strands of sea grass. Then he swiveled to the targets—and froze, hard as a side of beef in a meat locker. The sight of the sparkling wedges of fin had paralyzed him. He stood hunched, jaw slack, rod unready. The Bonefish Freeze.

Leaning into the pushpole, Skip kicked the stern to one side to insure Ken an unhindered shot. "Put one on 'em!" he prodded, to jolt the guy from his trance. He waited.

Skip knew first timers would often go into a stall and forget to cast—standing there, gaping at the bonefish like they had just seen a ghost. True enough, some folks called them "gray ghosts of the flats" and Skip figured they had earned the name. Spook people, hell, half the time bonefish spooked themselves. *Albula vulpes*, so full of foxiness they'd run from imaginary hounds. Which gave stunned anglers a mere sliver of time to make their casts before the bonefish felt the intensity of their gaze and squirted toanother longitude. Fishermen overwhelmed by the sight of them, frozen with astonishment, often squandered those crucial seconds.

Skip stressed urgency. "Ken! Hurry! Now! Lay it on him!"

Ken's epoxy fly sang through the air, carving a lofty arc. Up, up, high as the proverbial elephant's ass. Ten feet of fly line and ten feet of leader. The Ten Man.

"Oh man!" Ken Ten moaned. He hastily regrouped, but flailed again with an equivalent, sad result.

The pack of mudding bonefish had almost reached the boat, and Skip tensed, knowing what came next. One moment the bones rooted along raising flour puffs of marl, plowing like dutiful suburbanites having a Lawn Boy weekend. Then they spotted the skiff—and snapped into one of their famous warp speed retreats.

"Now that's acceleration," Skip drawled. "Damn near lost their scales, getting out of here."

Ken watched the blunt-veed bulge scream across the flat, gulped, "Sorry."

Skip began to amend his love of summer. His anglers struggled harder for hookups on these perfect, calm days, more so than when even a light breeze riffled the water. Partly because the fish acted spookier, since the smooth water gave them an unrippled window through which to see, or imagine, danger. And partly because when an angler saw a bonefish standing on its head his casting often turned to the hershey squirts. Call it stage fright or buck fever, Skip had watched even big name fishing pros suffer from it, and had been there himself more than once. Ken seemed like a decent sort, he just needed to steady himself, and try to get in a little practice.

Skip swung down from the poling platform. "Hey, how about I help you some with your distance."

Ken welcomed the offer. So Skip, with the zeal of a dedicated teacher, started to ease Ken's movements into the proper rhythm of snap and flow. He fervently wanted Ken to hook up, share the taste of that rush, the joy a hard sprinting bone could bring to the human spirit. He felt that many anglers underestimated bonefish, didn't realize how it took a hunter's attitude to successfully stalk the nervous creatures. And consequently many anglers arrived unprepared. Despite their contrary ways and the frustrations they provided him and his clients, Skip truly respected the bottom-grubbing little bone dogs.

After Ken's quick primer on the basic mechanics of the double haul, Skip resumed his watch from the tower. Plenty of time remained to score Ken a bonefish. He felt good about the day so far, but then, who wouldn't? The heavy air scented his lungs from a crayon-box array of tropical trees, all blooming with their flowered shouts for hummingbirds. Sweet as his wife Shelly's perfume. He gave a moment to thinking about how long her hair might have shimmered with those new glints before he got around to noticing its luster. A good thing they spent more time together in the summer. Of course that meant he ran fewer charters, so the trade-off reduced the glow a bit. Fish hard, then starve. Yeah. One of the penalties paid for the joy of having no boss was having no paid vacation. Or insurance, or retirement, or sick leave. When folks commented wistfully on what a great life he had, being a guide, he always thought, *Yeah, it's a great life if you don't weaken.* He poled toward a big wake, a nice push of fish.

Misfortune arrived.

In a deep channel beyond the flat a large boat advanced in wooden awkward racket. Skip wondered why in the hell it decided to head straight for him. He decided he must have an invisible magnet attached to his skiff, like a bullseye, the way he could be the only damn boat in sight, miles of water, the whole damn ocean, and here comes some Big Bertha Barge squeezing up into his skinny water. He waved his arms at the two guys standing on the noisy tub, to warn them away from the shallows and maybe, with luck, keep them from scaring every living thing off this flat. In water this depth their barge looked absurd—like the Queen Mary trying to float in a rain puddle.

The two guys waved back, but their gestures implied an attitude of, "Blow me, pal. We'll go where we bleepin' want." They gobbled words that sounded chewed from a dictionary and spoken backwards.

"Enjoy the show," Skip told Ken, "because fishing on this flat is now history. Before we even get a chance to scream at any goddam renegade jet skiers."

Skip felt at liberty with Ken to verbally slam jet ski jerkoffs. He had already gauged Ken's position, using the gradient that he had dreamed up over the years and dubbed the Peck Scale—One represented a dude who would rather lose the shot of a lifetime than challenge an interloper. Ten on the scale described a guy so confrontational he would just as soon punch out the lights of any intruder, no matter how innocent. In Skip's experience it was important that a guide decode this information about a client promptly, so as not to embarrass the client or make him nervous by leaning too far one way. Skip judged Ken at a solid takes-no-nonsense Six.

Ken smirked, "Speaking of them, last night I actually heard a bunch at the tiki bar call themselves jet pilots."

"Yeah. Ego poisoning." Skip snorted. He didn't mind the handful of law abiding ones all that much, because they puttered around and stayed out of the way, off the flats. Still noisy, though. But the more numerous rogues would jump the boat wakes of skiffs when they ran through

channels, got off on zooming circles around flats fishermen, and splashing spray on astonished clients while they
tried to bonefish. *Hotdog pukes who rooster-tailed the
shallows and ruined the fishing with their chest-beating
pretensions at manliness.* He had tried to rally fellow
members of the local guide's association to protest these
abuses and demand enforcement of existing laws, but they
had made scant headway so far. The term, "lack of manpower" kept arising.

Meanwhile, the guys in BB Barge proceeded. Their
Barge bogged; they revved her. She bogged harder and
stuck. Finally they splashed into the knee-deep water and
shoved in vain at two tons of brand-new shipwreck. "Garble garble," they waved at Skip. A new spirit of friendship
seemed to have expanded in their hearts.

Skip laughed. No kids were marooned aboard the tub,
and no dangers to life loomed ahead, other than the bore-
dom of waiting for the towboat. He poled off the flat to
leave them to their very predictable fate.

Wind born of speed pressed his polarized shades hard
against the bridge of his nose, the skiff hissed across the
turquoise saltwater to another spot. Skip considered the
juicy ticket and hefty towing fee in Two Guys' future when
the water cops fined them for grounding their boat in a
marine sanctuary. Might even tack some on for damaging
the sea grass. Yeah. He throttled back, lessening the roar of
his outboard, to relate a local legend about an assface who
had burned another guide in a similar way. Only worse.

"A while back, some slimeball ran smack dab in front
of where this guide bud of mine and his client were poling.
Had to show off his new flats boat along with his ignorance,
I guess. They waved him off, tried to keep some space to
fish, but the slime yelled insults, flipped them his I.Q.
Rude, on top of scumming them."

Ken nodded, swearing in agreement as he wiped away wind tears.

"Rumor had it he was a part-timer, which in the Keys we need like more mosquitoes. The kind of bloodsucker who earns solid bucks at a cushy job, so no problem affording their hobby boats, and no worry trying to pay a mortgage from charter fees. One of Them, the parasitic buttheads," Skip spat for emphasis, "takes just enough trips to keep half a dozen of us shy of a decent living. Wannabes, heads stuffed up there in the dark watching movies starring themselves. Heroes."

Ken sympathized. "Real assholes, huh?"

"Yeah. Anyway, the guide hairy eyeballed this parasite's boat. Day's end he went looking and found the boat docked, so he waited until the night settled down, until it got good and dark as the notion that had clutched his heart. Then he towed the rude guy's boat out into Florida Bay, far. You know, there's nothing much out there, just miles of skinny water and tiny islands with roosting herons and white-crowned pigeons. Well, he motored on out to Downtown Nowhere and pulled the plug on vermin's boat. Then he headed back home and slept the sleep of the righteous."

Ken's eyes went round. "I thought the days of piracy were over, except maybe on Wall Street."

Skip smiled. No extra charge for the thrills.

At the next flat Ken won the gold medal, the epitome of flats fly-fishing. Skip knew many anglers who had spent years in fruitless pursuit before achieving this summit, practicing their skills, braving wind, sun, and lockjawed fish. And then you have the guys you should hire to buy your lottery tickets.

From the mangrove shoreline seven white ibis kept score while a cloud drifted across the sun, wiping Skip cool with its breeze. A chop-flop of tiny wavelets hull-slapped the skiff, so he angled into them to dampen the noise. Sheets of sweat had already started sogging his tee shirt and he had to admit the breeze and the shadow felt good, though he felt half guilty having a nice thought about a cloud. Seemed most days clouds had it in for him. A summer squall would march its gray flannel blur across the water and chase him toward shelter, its electric wall of rain looking like a screen of bunny fur as it blocked access to the flat. Or a regiment of puffy cumulus would line up and track between him and the sun for hours, making it hard to spot fish. A hundred yards away the water would sparkle with yellow beams of fishing visibility. He'd move and the loyal clouds would follow. Skippy's little goddam lambs.

"See that wake? Ten o'clock! Point your rod! Left! Left!" Skip called Ken to attention, thinking, *Too many digitals in the world*. Ken had lapsed into that favorite of tiring anglers, clock hand amnesia. People truly fascinated Skip. Some would take it even further and pick a certain time quadrant, say nine, or two, and then expect fish to appear only right there and nowhere else, despite all evidence to the contrary. Spend, hell, *waste*, time staring into a desert of barren water. Film at eleven. He tried again. "See the lump in the water? Turn your head!"

"Oh! Yeah, that's a shark isn't it?"

"Permit! Cast! Now!" Skip commanded, encouraged, begged. Permit were masters of deceit. They could fool anyone with their lazy tail wag of a shark imitation. And when you got a shot at one you took it, bonefish fly be damned.

Ken cast.

Stars stopped rotating through galaxies and the jagged pieces of life's infinite puzzle tinkled into place. It all came together in one perfect moment as Ken did it right. Made it happen. The kind of moment fly fishermen live for, dream about. The fly line soared, homed toward the target, the tan Clouser landed, plink, into the water, the shadow gleamed toward it.

"Strip it!" Ken stripped.

"Wait!" Ken waited.

From the azure brine a flash of silver shot out between fins lit fluorescent black. The permit found the fly and wiggled like a puppy for a bone. Woofed it.

And Ken tightened line as directed, and a solar burst of anger beamed from the permit. It warped toward a new dimension. A hundred feet out it paused, then turned sideways to take advantage of its disc shape. Its fins went brown with disgust. Although not even a favored crab fly something about it must have resembled a yummy morsel, and now the Fooler hated being fooled.

Skip humped the skiff after the retreating permit to keep Ken from getting spooled. The blood sang in his veins, songs of hearty congratulations and generous tips. Not that he thought of himself as a venal money-grubber, though. Not at all. He believed that the whole point of his job was for fishermen to step off his skiff at the end of the day tired, sun-browned, and happy about the bonefish, permit, or tarpon they had seen or caught. Enthused about sighting some flamingoes, or spotted eagle rays, or bottlenose dolphin with their iodine smiles. He considered it his duty as a guide. If accumulating stacks of money drove his life he'd wear a tie and a greasy smile behind a desk somewhere. Wouldn't he? Still, old Ken's cods would probably swell up big enough to sling over his shoulder after this exploit. Have to load 'em up in a wheelbarrow when they got back to the dock. Skip loved permit. For a lot of reasons, actually, but hell, some guys tipped big when they caught permit, especially on fly. Maybe he could take Shelly out to dinner, make up for the lean times lately, or buy her something lacy. Yeah.

Ken gained line, reeling and panting, his dress code angler uniform wet a shade darker at contact points. "This fish is stronger than me," he gasped.

"You're doing good. He's closer, try to get his head up. Tires him out. We want to get him to the boat without hurting him." Skip tolerated no fish abuse.

The permit materialized like dreamshine, motes of its form fluttering into view through translucence. Pale yellow flanks and mirrors. Now it portrayed its fins as dull slate brackets around its anger; not its day at all. A mad moon on the rise.

Skip leaned over the gunwale and grasped it at the wrist of its forked tail, cradled its blunt head with his other hand, breathed deep of its ocean fresh scent. "Damn, Ken! He must be close to twenty. You outdid yourself!" He placed its satin body back in the water, hands from another world moving the amazed fish back and forth through alternate realities. Its smart eyes rolled up at him. This permit would have tales to tell that Gulliver could believe. "Your camera ready?" A man never has too many permit pictures.

"He's a pretty nice fish," Ken remarked. After the photo session he watched the ethereal creature glide toward a secret corner of the deep to pout.

Skip thought Ken sounded a little lackluster about this monumental event. Perhaps he didn't understand his incredible luck. "A miracle catch, no lie. I mean—your first day ever saltwater fly-fishing, the first permit you've ever seen, the first time you throw at one—and you even landed it! Didn't even have a crab fly tied on! Man, some guys'd give their left nut for that fish!"

"Really? I'd still like to catch a bonefish though."

An uneasy feeling grabbed a fistful of Skip's gut. *What if Ken really didn't comprehend what he had just accomplished? Naw, he was a fun guy, up to date, aware. He probably knew that though permit might be easy enough to feed in deep water over wrecks, or with live crabs, they seldom ate flies all that well, especially on the flats. He was just numb from the shock. It hadn't hit him yet, but when it did he'd flash. Yeah.* Skip cut short his brooding and answered Ken's plaintive remark with his usual optimism. "Sure thing. Bonefish should be easier for you now that you've conquered a wary permit." *Wrong.*

So he headed the skiff toward a flat where the resident bonefish showed up black against the olive-drab tones of the grass, to make it easy for Ken to spot them. Skip had found that in some areas bonefish tended to look transparent green, in others they looked as faint as a cloud, almost colorless, but on a few flats they appeared black across their backs. Oddly enough, when you pulled them up close to the boat you could see that they each wore the same silver sides shaded with olive green diamonds, along with that cool ice blue edging on their fins. But from a distance, greenish, black, or vague as smoke. Remarkable creatures.

On the way to the flat he considered, *What if this day turned out like that time with the honeymooners. . . .*

Nice kids, also new to saltwater fishing. Once Skip had realized that the husband qualified as legally flats blind and that the wife seemed determined to catch the glass minnows hovering under the boat, once he figured all that out, things went well. Really, they did. When Mr. looked right through a bonefish school as big as a garage, not even seeing the mud streaking off their backs in eloquent plumes, Skip had to invent a whole new tactic. And it worked like a charm. Mr. hooked up to a zingy little bonefish right away—about the size of a banana, but it pulled like a locomotive. Then Skip used the same method when neither angler saw the assembled black fins of a school of permit, loafing, floating on the surface. That time the technique worked so well that both Mr. and Mrs. hooked and landed permit. At the same time. A double. Even with spin fishermen it counted as phenomenal. But despite the success of their day and Skip's above and beyond efforts, Mr. and Mrs. had appeared unmoved. Back at the dock, handshakes and polite smiles emerged, and the requisite thanks for a wonderful time. But not even a token tip. He believed his unflagging thoroughness had exceeded that of a measly poling machine fueled by greenbacks. Forget the sweat and the soul, just put five bucks in the meter for fifteen minutes. The slight had stung. Still, he recognized that lots of people lived on a tight budget, like he and Shelly. *So maybe Mr. and Mrs. should have stayed in a hotel that didn't cost four big ones a night*, his cranky inner voice snapped back.

At the next bonefish flat Ken developed innovative tricks that stretched the imagination, novel ways to blow a cast. He had started acting a little tired before the permit, now his concentration dribbled away like a leaky dick. He wanted to sit down. He wanted to get a drink from the cooler and slam the lid.

"Gives 'em confidence," Skip said after the second cooler slam. He suspected Ken had achieved that too-much-sun, burnt-out state clients reached now and then, their attention as skittery as water drops on a hot skillet. Being out here could sometimes suck the juice from your bones.

Ken finally fired off a decent cast at a hungry, hard working bone, but then suddenly yanked the fly out of its suction-popping little lips. "These fish won't eat," he proclaimed.

Skip laughed, made the crack, "Yeah, must be going through their Gandhi phase. Funny though, a guy last week said the same thing. He'd fished for years, stripers and blues up north, thought of himself as pretty salty. But I guess those bluefish he's used to catching are so aggressive they'd hook themselves on a rowboat's oarlocks if your lure didn't get in the way."

Ken snickered.

"Our finicky bones down here showed him how fishing these flats differed from what he'd done before. Said he felt like he was back in kindergarten."

"Me, too."

The faint splosh from the pushpole filled in between Skip's laughter and comments and grunts of effort. He loved this pole, over twenty feet of graphite lightness; his stylus, printing his ephemeral mark on the flats of time. Tracing his life through turtle grass and sargassum.

"I'd really like to catch a bonefish," Ken repeated.

Skip wished he'd catch one, too, then maybe he'd get off his back about it, remember that he had actually caught the pinnacle, the prize of the flats, the transcendent permit. "Okay, let's try something new on the next one."

"What's that?"

"Let's not see who can get to the boat first, your fly or the fish. Remember, it's not a race. So try letting the poor little sucker wrap his lips around the fly before you set up."

Ken chuckled at his own antsy habit. "Guess I'm pretty nervous still."

"Yeah. Maybe you could just pretend it's a shark," Skip suggested, since it had worked so well when Ken cast to the permit.

But all Ken's pretending and all Skip's poling and urging only brought them to late afternoon. The light slanted across the water in a dazzling yellow glare. Skip moved to a flat where the lowering sun shone behind them and they had the right stage of the tide. The flat sparkled barren and fishless. Skip wondered if this acreage, this usually bountiful bonefish grazing land had already been swept clean by anonymous screaming heathens in shallows-running frenzies. If so, no use fishing in propwash. He moved again, went around the world, and back, poled faster and harder, the way guides always do when they have trouble getting their clients a fish. But he couldn't hurry, pole, or finagle a bonefish onto Ken's hook.

Only so many days fit in an hour and the end of this day's hours had arrived.

Well, Skip mused, as they sped through swamp fusty mangrove creeks on their way back to the dock, *the day had still turned out decent.* Ken had appreciated the humor when he used the wrong fly on a pod of bonefish and the bones had laughed their asses off all the way across the flat. And the bigger joke when he'd tied on a surefire fly and the bonefish still wouldn't eat. Wrong fly, right fish. Then right fly, wrong fish—or maybe wrong retrieve. He had chuckled at the clownish antics of a trunkfish, and again when a barracuda had severed his leader and he lost his pricey epoxy fly. Then he had caught that permit— great for a first timer, a fish with size to it, to boot.

Skip relished the hot breeze against his sodden tee shirt and thought about prime rib. He had only managed a couple bites of his bologna sandwich and the old Skippy brand poling motor now sat on walk. Shelly would probably want to go for something exotic for her dinner out, like Thai food. Or, wait, maybe they should order in, get Chinese, or pizza, save the rest for that lacy thing. Yeah.

"I had a lot of fun," Ken said. Rumpled but smiling, he waited on the dock while Skip unloaded his tackle bag from the dry storage compartment.

Grinning back, Skip said, "Yeah, hope those pictures turn out for you."

"I'll send you one, if they do. I sure hope I can get back down here and do this again sometime soon. Maybe a few days during tarpon season. It's been great fishing with you, telling stories and stuff; I learned a lot. The best vacation I've had in years." Ken stuck out his hand.

Skip shook it. "Be glad to have you back on my boat."

"Thanks. Oh, uh, here. Here's my card, and a check for what I owe you. Thanks again." Ken picked up his gear and walked to his car.

Skip flicked his eyes to the card, the check under it, glanced casually at the numbers. Furtively, to be polite, but unable to restrain his curiosity or curb his racing brain from its plans of gourmet food and satin nights. Stopped. Looked up. Smiled real slow at Ken's distant figure closing his car door with that solid chonk you hear on the best of the priciest.

His mind throbbed like a hammered thumb. Yeah. No tip.

ELEVEN

 *Poles Apart*

Slosh. Tinkle. Tinkle. Skip shot the foot of the pushpole into the salt muck bottom of Florida Bay and swore under his breath. Damn thing had a leak. Now, waterlogged, it seemed to weigh as much as a case of outboard oil. Made poling even more aerobic. Snake bit in Snake Bight. The joys of summer in the Everglades—a bald eagle's soft whistle, the ravenous slash of a feeding snook, the piggy grunts of alligators—dimmed and blurred. Even his client's delight at fighting his third toy-sized tarpon to the skiff didn't help. It only served to accent the gap between image and reality in his life lately. The magic of fish that shine like quicksilver contrasted with the thought of another fun evening taking this pushpole apart and trying to fix it. It could sour your mood.

This would be the, what? Fourth, fifth try? Hell, he'd lost count. When it first came up he called around to guys he knew had done it before. See what they knew. Everyone had a different story: "Epoxy," said one. "Marine Tex is the only way," said two. "Be sure to plug it with closed cell foam first," advised three.

Skip had driven all over town on his "day off" looking for the right brand of epoxy. At about the last store in the world he found it, went home—after stopping to borrow a friend's miter box—and commenced. The pole had looked good when he finished, and he hadn't had any trouble putting it together, except for when the ant lion bit him. Guess he'd been kneeling on its small silt crater. He had balanced the pole carefully where the wind wouldn't disturb it and used his newer backup pushpole the next day while it dried.

He should have known that day held adversity when he met his angler. Guy came on friendly enough, all right. So friendly that he wouldn't stop talking long enough to hear Skip's advice, like to string his rod. Be ready. But he had talked right over the words, stuffed the bare rod in the rack, put two bulging bags of gear into the dry storage compartment. Didn't miss a syllable. First thing, his hat blew off. With a cringe at the frittered time Skip swung the skiff back around and scooped the straw sombrero out of the water. Give it that salty look, yeah. Maybe if you wear a hat like this, the tide waits for you.

When they reached the flat, little terns swooped in the hazy peach sky and the water lay soft. Skip said, "Okay, I'm going to pole along this edge here until we see the first tails, the tide's perfect, so any second the bonefish will. . . ." Then he stopped in disbelief.

Motorlips kept bubbling out inanities while unboxing, oh yes, unboxing, a brand new reel. Thing didn't even have backing on it.

"Hey," Motor asked, "how do you get this stuff on here?"

At least he had brought some backing. So Skip staked the boat, wound on the backing, took the brand new fly line out of its box, tied the nail knot, tied up a leader, and tied on an epoxy fly. All the time listening to Motor tell him how best to do it, all the time his peripheral warning systems sounding alarms: Tails, Tails, Tails. "I think you're ready now," he said with great restraint, and handed Motor the strung rod.

The day went okay after that. As well as a day can after you've wasted the best of the morning tide. Motor settled down and started making reasonable casts. Thirty, forty footers, but fairly accurate. Surprised and pleased, Skip started thinking to himself that maybe he had judged the guy too fast. They boated and released a six pounder; a cruiser that glommed the fly even after Motor had beaned him. One of those heaven-sent sea carp given to moments of poor judgement.

With the pressure off, Skip fell into a good rhythm. Stroking up the flat, the faintest wind cooling him, he scanned the water for the next push of fish. Though this pole weighed mere ounces, its surface didn't have the same familiar texture as his old favorite. The difference, the scratchiness, niggled at him. He hated the distraction. Bonefishing was a pursuit based on concentration. The squawk of an angry heron rang through the heavy salt air in agreement.

Then Skip felt his expensive all-graphite backup pushpole give way. He had leaned on it hard to spin the skiff toward the wake of some cruising bonefish. Damn. He pulled it up. Cracked at the base of the foot. Overpriced piece of dog meat. Now this one would get water in it, too. Maybe just a little today, but ruin had it marked. Just like a gypsy mark on the door of a future burglary victim, nothing good lay in store for this pole. What was going on? Had he not held his mouth right? Angered the pushpole gods? How long would this curse keep chewing on him?

He used the re-glued one the next day. It leaked. Slosh, tinkle, tinkle, with every move. He stopped at a tackle shop on the way back from the boat ramp, bought a new foot for the new pole and a new ferrule for the old pole. Bought some new sections, too, one all graphite, one graphite composite. Because every time he cut into a pole it lost length. Went home, called a bud and asked if he could borrow his push-pole for tomorrow's charter. "Sure, it'll be in the backyard by the fence. We won't be home, so just ignore the dogs."

Yeah. Skip personally loved dogs, animals in general. But he wasn't about to go into this guy's yard when the two very large mouths presented themselves at the gate. Bark-ing, snarling. Dogs looked like black rugs with teeth. He had just begun to shuffle away, defeated, when their neigh-bor, out watering his mango tree, intervened. "They're all talk," he joked, and came on over and patted the two now slobbery wall-to-wall heads while Skip nabbed the push-pole. It wasn't the kind he liked to use. Too short, too flex-ible, and too heavy. What was this guy doing with a limp dick cheapo fiberglass pole anyway? But what the hell, he was out of options.

On his next "day off" he fought his way again through the heavy traffic on the Overseas Highway; tourists in red or white clone cars twisting their necks and driving 20 miles under the limit. He looked for closed cell foam, found something like it in a craft shop after several stops earned him blank expressions. Clerks giving him the empty space behind the eyes look—"You want what?" And Marine Tex; he bought the industrial sized package. Spent the rest of the afternoon repairing the two push-poles. Again. Carefully.

In the morning he found the Marine Tex had failed to set up. Skip wiped off the congealed mess and sagged onto the nearby doorstep. Listened to the faint whine of a mosquito hunting for a landing strip on his leg. Looked like the pushpole factory guy would be kept busy repairing poles now that old Skipper had got the hang of ruining the damn things. Yeah. And he'd have to use his friend's wet noodle of a stick until they were fixed. He felt jaded, faded, and, like his old Grandpa would tersely phrase it, as useless as tits on a boar.

Shelly came outside, down the steps. She glanced at the wadded paper towels full of uncured glop, at the pushpoles and parts at Skip's feet. She sat down by him. He noticed that she smelled good, like cookies. "Hmm, time to buy another one, huh?" she murmured.

His heart slipped a gear. Man, she was amazing. "That'd make three," he said. "Cost a couple charters."

"Good looks, math ability, what a guy." She grinned at him, teasing, her eyes full of light and promise. "We'll call it the 'By now it's a real emergency' backup pole." Flashed that smile that pulled him together when he felt stretched way out. Flicked the mosquito off his knee. Before it bit.

TWELVE

 The Same Wrong Thing

Monofilament boiled off the reel spool. The shrimp splashed into the jade sea broth and kicked for safety, bolting for cover in the turtle grass.

"Close your bail!" Skip warned.

Despite the "seabreeze" of Gale Lite velocity a pod of bonefish had tailed up. Their caudals winked like spilled sequins in the bright Florida Keys sun.

Skip's fisherman panicked. "What's a bail?" quavered the hapless intern. Dr. Snarfle.

Laughter gargled Skip's answer, "The skinny metal arch above the spool. Spool holds the line."

Guiding, Skip had fished enough doctors to grow wary; if infirmity struck he'd sooner eat chum than consult one about health. If they tended to their medicine like his client doctors tended to take direction, winning millions from magazine giveaways made a safer bet. It also put him skittish when a surgeon showed a singular lack of eye-hand coordination; that seemed a surefire booking to the dirt nap hotel.

"It's tangled now," Doc delivers. Helpful guy.

Down from the poling platform, which a few of his charters had called "that roof over your motor," Skip cut the snarl, retied the hook. Forget that surgeon's knot myth. Guys probably use super glue these days.

"You're ready. Now, when you see a mud, cast into it." Skip gave up on scheduling Doc and bonefish tails into the same operation. He decided to pin his hopes on muds, the upwellings of roiled marl caused by feeding bonefish. Those made a target big enough for even the precision impaired. Usually.

"Got it." Doc stood tall, squinted through his sunglasses. "What mud?"

"You sure those are polarized?" *Maybe he couldn't tell the difference, it happens a lot.* "Here, let me." Skip peered. The surface film of the knee-deep seaweed soup formed a glare barrier. *No way.* "Okay Doc, stuff these." Skip fetched a spare pair from his dry box. So many clients wrongly thought their high-dollar designer glasses were polarized that he always kept a backup pair on hand. Hard to sight fish if you can't see. "Try 'em."

"Wow!" Doc marveled. "I see the bottom! Look! Is that a bonefish?"

"Barracuda."

"Can I catch him?"

"You can try. But use the rod with the wire leader."

"Oh. Maybe I'll land a bonefish first then."

And maybe that Publisher's Giveaway van will park in my driveway. But Skip said, "Okay. Let's do it. Remember, don't hold your rod tip too high or there's nowhere to go when you set the hook."

From the vantage point of the tower he mused, *We'll spot muds here soon; the bonefish tend to cluster in this grass.* Then his mind drifted to statistics, probabilities. Laughing gulls swooped in the warm salt-filled air, made fun as insight eluded him. Waves slapped the hull, so he angled the skiff on a tangent. He puzzled over how his motley array of fishermen could all manage to do the Same Wrong Things, consistently. How could this happen? Did they commune by hidden signals? How else to explain the marvel that somehow allowed them all to choose the wrong option? Common sense expected birdies as often as bogeys, but life revealed a sandtrap. Daily, clients would board his skiff, *then* apply sunscreen. Doc did. Why didn't, just by chance, half of them swab on their unguents at the hotel? Hell, it says to apply *before* exposure right on the tube. There, they could see amusing glops left in amazing spots. They could wash their hands, removing stench and residue so they wouldn't taint fly lines, flies, or bait. Or, for the most fun, eyes. Instead, five minutes into their smear campaign he'd hear the cry, "Oowww, my eyes are stinging. What should I do?" *Read the label comes to mind.*

And tackle. Why bother to tie on that Clouser's minnow *before* the skiff whooshed down at the first flat? As if they couldn't possibly see any bonefish until, knots pulled tight, drinks sipped and replaced, snacks duly tasted and pocketed, they felt that deep inner readiness. Yeah. As if their guide had burned a steak dinner's worth of fossils in his outboard to gain this point, at this hour, on this tide, on a mission less urgent than bone stalking.

And on to rain gear. Those clients who actually thought to bring some (Hey, we're going to the subtropics, do you think it might rain?), frequently left it in their motel room. Very handy there, keep that closet dry. Those who remembered to pack rainwear in their gear bags, more often than not, only brought the jacket. Skip had finally asked one guy, "So, you suppose it will only rain on you from the waist up?"

Doc's cool though, grasps the humor in his bumble-hood. Besides, I like laughing, next to fishing. Lucky me. "Okay, see the mud bloom at twelve o'clock?"

Doc faced ten-thirty. He favored that quadrant. "No-oo-oo."

"Twelve. Two hundred feet."

"Still not." Doc turned, perplexed that his complex mind full of boney parts and bacteria names couldn't solve this bonefish problem.

Skip chuckled. Doc remained focused on ten-thirty. "Point your rod. Out in front of you. Yeah. Okay, come right, right. There." Thankfulness buoyed him. He had fished a pair of greenhorns last week who could not figure out how to point their rods. They tried overhead, sideways, every way but out. Imagine.

"Wow! Look at that murky place!"

"That's the mud. Bonefish footprints."

"I'm ready."

"Drop your shrimp a little." Doc liked to reel the shrimp right up into the tip guide. Rod looked like it was pooping shrimp. "Yeah, open the bail but hold onto the line. Good. Now we're going to creep up on them. Remember, throw fast or they'll boogie."

Few anglers, fly or spin, realized the importance of speed when bonefishing. Especially stream fishermen, accustomed to having light years to pitch McGintys onto a trout's place mat. But bonefish ramble around, shopping for their groceries. Wait too long and they would shop at another mall, leaving you all baited up and nowhere to throw.

Skip praised the day. Not the irksome poling-into-the-wind factor, which literally blew, and butt chunks at that, but what this irksome wind had spared him. In a fit of expanded imagination, Doc had booked this as a fly-fishing trip. Only last night, on the phone after hearing the weather conjecture, had he admitted his lack of casting skill in windy conditions. Witness now to his flair with spinning gear, Skip would venture Any Tackle, Any Conditions. Skip believed fly-fishing added to the flavor of challenge. But since the pursuit of bonefish employed the same tactics of stalking and sight casting whether fishing fly or spin, either method satisfied his hunter's nature. Hence and thankfully, today no weighted flies whizzed by his head on rookie-generated ear piercing forays.

Reminded him of that time a guide friend had his ear pierced by a guy who insisted that he was a good caster. Wind? Sure, I can handle it. Even after he noticed it, his friend had left the barb on this angler's hook. He *always* fished barbless but on this one day he wavered, not heeding that little voice, "self." Soon thereafter Self found himself at the local emergency room, enduring a hook extraction. Skip had thrilled to two recent face hits himself, his angler's fly crashing smack into Skip's thank god double tough sunglasses. The juice of life dwells in the details.

"Okay Doc, house mud, wing one."

Doc hurled his shrimp toward Belize.

"Reel in, quick, try again."

Doc froze, befuddled.

"The handle on the reel, turn it, fast!" Skip eased down, grabbed another shrimp, to have it ready when the hook arrived.

Sweat popped on Doc's lip. He slung the new bait at the mud.

"Tighten up on your line. Feel for him, feel for him."

"Wow, it's stuck. Oh! Hey!"

A young bonefish, about the length of a nice Bluefield banana, had spied the shrimp feast as it jerked erratically through his turf. With tarpon aspirations he flared his shadowy pectorals, surged forward, and slurped it into rubbery white lips. Yum! Ouch! Seeeee Ya.

"Ya HOO!" Skip cheered. "When he stops running, pump up and reel down." He started planning on how to spend that ten million.

"He's taking a lot of thread!" Doc gasped.

"Line. Unless you're stitching." Overall, Doc didn't give the impression of being all that naïve, but in terms of fishing, yeah, greener than a golf course. "Lift up on the rod, now drop the tip down, fast! and *crank* that handle!" Pump up and reel down obviously a foreign language here. "No. No! That's better. Don't lose the rhythm. He's getting tired."

"*I'm* getting tired," Doc laughed. He kept winding against the drag, and confusing pump/lift with drop/reel.

But the bonefish had torched through those shrimp calories on his blitz across the flat. Closer now, close enough to see his startled eyes of amber and black, with their typical Oh! Oh! bonefish expression. Somehow he looked embarrassed. Skip reached over and scooped him out, saying "Good job, good job," as much to him as to Doc. Droplets sparkled, dripping from his sides, and Skip noticed anew that bonefish smelled a little like lawn clippings.

Doc leaned the rod against the cooler. Skip riveted his attention on this Right Thing for an incredulous instant. So often when clients hustled over to admire their catch, his rods dropped like the barometer in a hurricane—crash! onto the deck. Could this mark the onset of a fresh new life in some new, alternate universe where The Same Right Things held sway? *Aw, what the hell, maybe I'm just being anal about all this stuff.* Doc grabbed his camera, chortled, "Wow, he's shiny."

"Here, wet your hands, give him water, I'll shoot the picture."

Doc smiled into the future. His skill as a hunter proven, no diagnosis could escape him now.

"Hold him until he kicks away," Skip advised. Doc, intent, revived the dismayed six-pounder. His shoulders, wrists, cheeks, all radiated care—a Doc in those awkward bones after all. "Ready to try for another one?"

He lifted his chin, beaming rapture, nodding yes. The bonefish wiggled; Doc relaxed his fingers and whistled as its white-striped silver flanks shimmered into green disappearance. "Wow. Awesome fish."

They persevered. But it seemed that Doc had consumed his daily dose of luck, and his bobbles began to worsen, toss after hurl. Still, back at the dock he chuckled, clapped Skip on the tricep a couple times *(just one day, and I'm spouting the jargon),* and said, "Man, that was fantastic. I had read stories about bonefish and they are wa-a-y beyond what I expected. Man, I've *got* to try them fly-fishing." He cracked up when Skip thanked him for the warning.

The last laugh, though, came at home, when Skip pulled the rods out from under the gunwales. Instead of into the *bridge of the line guide,* Doc had carefully fastened each hook on each rod into the *eye* of the line guide—where it can nick the eye. Nicked eyes fray line. Skip's world remained safely twisted in its same warped universe. Like damn near everyone before him, Doc had done The Same Wrong Thing.

THIRTEEN

The Bonefish Imperative: Blaze of Feathers

For the road less traveled, the water less fished.
Of endless poling, with swollen ankles and sun baked meat.
Thrift bound by sacrifice on the altar of
Skiff, Outboard, Reel, and Rod.
Driven from the clamor of man, to seek virgin
sites to cast a line.
Forsaking security, comfort, for the thrill of cutlass
fins that pierce the water.
For the hookup. For the sizzling run. For the Bonefish.

Shelly could imagine it embroidered, framed. Maybe shorten it some, but keep the essence. "The Bonefish Imperative." It felt like a compelling force in their life, but she couldn't tell whether it had more power in the past or future. Not a bad life, mind you, but unique. It made her think of that Irish imprecation, *May you have an interesting life*. Or was that a Chinese curse? Gypsy?

Whenever she read books, stories, she found herself trying to pry up the surface, peer underneath, the way you might a damaged fingernail, hoping to determine the cause. She sought the character behind the words, the realm from which they wrote this attempt to influence her thoughts. So, what would Skip think if he read this sketch of her vision?

She sighed and looked away from her notebook. Outside in the soupy hot afternoon, a typical Florida Keys summer day kept the AC humming. A gray squirrel sprawled on a branch of the gumbo limbo tree next to their house. Pinky. Poised like a sphinx, she fluffed her tail in the breeze from the AC unit's fan. This friendly mother squirrel with translucent pink ears would pat Shelly's hand with her soft pink pads, whenever Shelly gave her a peanut. Eurasian collared doves, lustrous as pearls, dribbled themselves around the yard, hopping like feathered basketballs; she hoped the big dummies wouldn't poop out any poisonwood seeds to take root. White-crowned pigeons and lots of the Keys birds liked those berries; Shelly did *not* like how contact with the tree made her skin boil.

Above her desk a shadow box graced the wall, framing eleven exquisite flies that Skip had tied. Traditional steelhead flies, ornate Atlantic salmon patterns, an innovative shrimp of his own creation. As the cozy rumble of thunderheads echoed from over Florida Bay, she glanced at his calligraphy, name and date on the bottom—had it really been that long? So many miles away, so many bonefish flats ago.

It seemed now to her that these feathered creations and the sleek animals they sought to trick had woven themselves into her destiny long before she had even finished her growth. Long before she realized someone named Skip would combine those elements into the material of her life.

Shelly stared harder, unable to decode the actions of the fisherman. From the rocky knoll where she sat astride a mulish stable horse named Blaze, she squinted far across a sun-glossed meadow. A stream sparkled through the elongated meadow, edged with bunchy plants, green as envy. She counted a half dozen people. From here they appeared the size of dragonflies as they fished for trout along the meander, her Mom and Dad among them. Pines behind her oozed resin, pungent from afternoon heat, and her ears resonated with the metallic buzz of cicadas.

The summer dust, like powder in the air from a stamp of Blaze's hoof, made her sniffle. She wiggled in the saddle. Her prepubescent eyeballs had at first doubted themselves, but it looked as if, okay, yes, her Dad, and a bird. It fluttered over his head, circling, high up, and—oh no! attached by the line from his fly rod!

It took a double thump of both heels, hard, on Blaze's ribs to rouse him from his oat dreams. Shelly's folks had rented this sorrel horse to entertain her while they fished, and she and Blaze had moseyed over rocky trails since lunchtime. While she dreamed of discovering rare minerals or a missing species or ancient artifacts, he plodded. He grunted now, flicking his cinnamon ears in pique, but soon enough they trotted and jounced downhill toward the drama of this puzzling scene. The dragonflies grew into adult humans.

"Daddy! How did you catch a bird?" Shelly slid from the saddle, reins in hand, and made a couple gangly skips to the heart of the bizarre.

"Watch out, honey, don't get tangled," warned her Mom. She approached from downstream carrying her rod, the hook dangling a sodden worm. She was deadly with worms. Shelly's Dad preferred to cast fluffy, colorful bits of feather and yarn with his fly rod. Shelly didn't know for sure who caught the most fish, but the way that fly line

curled over him, as scrolled and loopy as her schoolgirl
cursive, sure looked neat. Like some secret language.

"Don't hurt it, Daddy, please!" Shelly pictured their
precious turquoise parakeet—lodging at her best friend
Linda's house this week, and probably squawking in
protest every time Linda practiced her accordion, who
wouldn't? This little bird, flapping and chirping overhead,
had brown tabby feathers like a sparrow or finch. Likely a
Mom then, with a nest full of yawning beaks to stuff with
worms. No, wait, she must have chased after bugs for her
lunch menu today, otherwise she wouldn't have somehow
caught her Daddy's Royal Coachman, or whatever, in mid-
cast. That was about *his* favorite bug.

By now all the birdy tumult had drawn attention to itself. A couple of the fishermen Shelly had seen scattered
along this idyllic, clear, cold stream, a tributary of the
Tuolumne River, straggled closer. They circled the center
of this fuss in the meadow and offered mutters of advice
and encouragement. An unexpected novelty amidst their
Sierra Nevada vacations.

"Nice fish," one guy joked. "Knock it inna head," said
the other. Although not Shelly's first inkling that people
could bristle with tactlessness, she cringed at the lout's
words. Gravity had suddenly released her stomach to float
in weightless dread of such an outcome. Shelly, even still,
disliked elevators.

As the other anglers along this stream most likely had,
Shelly's family had toured the awesomely beautiful
Yosemite Valley. This hearkens back to what seemed now
to her like olden days, when a passenger car was still allowed to roam the scenic route at a driver's will. They had
then settled into a rental cabin by a lake down canyon
from Yosemite, off towards Mono Lake. Such lakes and

streams lay sprinkled and twisted throughout these rugged mountains, and her folks spent every day, dawn to dusk, fishing deliriously. At night, from motley crockery on a red-checked oilcloth, they ate crispy fried trout dredged in cornmeal, canned pork 'n' beans, and sliced tomatoes or ears of fresh corn. Outside, nothing but pine wind quiet and billions of stars like Tinkerbelle's fairy dust.

Although intoxicated with everything about the Sierras—from its sweet, sharp air and secret animal tracks to the piebald rocks on its streambottoms—the actual catching of these rainbow-enhanced fish had yet to capture Shelly's spirit. Her folks, it seemed, managed to eke out little enough time to indulge themselves in their passion for fishing. Consequently, they rarely squandered much of these precious opportunities to force-feed her a regimen of angling instructions. And who could blame them, since she would normally reward their sincere attempts with her ephemeral span of attention—before galloping off on another make-believe jaunt. At any rate, her sympathies remained solidly with the fish.

When asked to accompany them along watery skirts of creeks or lakes in earlier years, her amused parents would find the creels left in her care full of living fish. Shelly kept their creels (the traditional woven willow kind with leather edges) submerged, the caught fish, whether trout or perch or bass, finning and gilling comfortably among the lily pads or horsetails, until the moment they headed back home. She often proffered stray bugs to her captives as rations, chiding her temporary pets when they refused their snacks. Why did they prefer some bugs over others? Consumed by that bottomless curiosity of kids, she experimented with beetles and flies and whatnot, and studied the responses seriously, as if she might understand them. Oddly enough, in

this juvenile version of incipient catch-and-release consciousness, Shelly experienced no qualms whatsoever at
dinnertime when her former charges appeared in their
crusty guise of cornmeal gold. Trout were, after all, food.

Older at the time of this vacation, she had come to consider horses as godlike creatures placed on this planet for
the adoration and delight of bumptious little girls with
bruise-prone shins. Hence, Blaze. Spoiled hayburner, her
Dad called him, with that one-way gear all rental horses
seem to possess—an ears-up gallop back toward the barn
and oats. Any direction away from barn and grain, that
equine paradise of food-enhanced inertia, brought out his
poutiest hoof-dragging walk. Possibly stable horses are
safer that way, at least going in one direction, with their
built-in governor that prevents youngsters from urging
them into a breakneck pace, and consequently falling off
and slamming into the ground. But it had taken concerted
vigorous kicking to urge Blaze into a reluctant trot to scope
out this bird emergency. While Blaze cropped meadow
grass at the end of his reins, Shelly began to realize, with
a measure of disillusionment, that the name Blaze must
have more to do with his bright cinnamon coat or his
white splashed face than his sizzling velocity.

"Here, honey." Shelly's Mom handed her Dad a red bandanna. She kept her poodle curly hair covered with it
while she fished, so it probably smelled like her citrusy
cologne. "Wrap her in this."

Shelly's Dad had by now stripped fly line back through
the guides on his rod, and had shortened tether enough on
the frightened bird to land it, so to speak. He eased the rod
down to the grass, holding just the tip and leader in one
hand, and stepped toward the fluffed, cheeping bird with
the red bandanna in the other.

And presto—small brown bird disappeared beneath big square cloth! Her Dad grabbed the bird with one rough calloused hand and Shelly squeezed her eyes shut for a second in fear that he would squish its tiny-boned body. Behind her eyes she pictured the horror of finding this little baked bird on her dinner plate, but when she opened them again (feeling a bit silly because she loved fried chicken and that was a bird, too) she saw the finch-bird wriggling, its tiny head bared. With the hook stuck through its beak. Shelly pushed her face as close as possible, fretful but trying to determine how this all had happened.

"Mother, hold her a minute while I cut the hook," her Dad said. And her Mom cocooned Finchie, who had quit fluttering, in both hands. He used shiny pliers and snipped the hook in two at its curve near her bill, and Shelly noticed it was that cute bee fly he called McGinty rather than the longer Coachman. The ruined fly and leader dropped to the ground. Shelly stuffed it, a talisman of release, into the pocket of her jeans. Then her Dad pulled the remaining piece of hook out the small hole pierced in the miniature beak.

At first Shelly amazed how his rough oilfield hands could perform such a delicate task, then memory kicked in. She recalled all those evenings during the winter months when he had hunched over the kitchen table, tying these flies. No conflict between size and dexterity, it appeared, and she filed that deduction away in her growing list of worldly observations. She supposed, now, if he had heard of barbless hooks he might have used them, but in those days that whole concept may not have yet emerged into popular practice. Or maybe he would have thought them frivolous, since they ate the fish that he and her Mom caught. Even so, they released those too small, and quit keeping them when they had enough. Shelly had never heard her father say the word karma, nor had he ever seemed to anguish over his own. He derived from that time and place, a location in our past, when more people lived closer to Nature and apparently didn't feel as if they defaced it by partaking of its bounty. Whichever side one now took on such issues had no impact on what he had conveyed: the calm confidence of dominion, along with the weight of all the commitment such a station implies.

"There, there," her Mom said, unwrapping the bandanna from the wide-eyed bird. Finchie's feathers were mussed, and she perched in her Mom's hand a few seconds longer, acting bewildered. A momentous ordeal, compared to her simple avian life. Then she fluffed herself out, round, like you see doves do on a cold morning, adjusted her wings, and hopped into the sky. She bee-lined toward the thick stand of pine trees that fringed the meadow, across the creek. Shelly felt the fist let go of her heart.

Her Dad reached into his shirt pocket and removed a sueded leather wallet, flopped it open. Nestled in rows, stuck in sheepskin, an array of buggy hooks awaited his decision. Relieved now, Shelly nosed closer to all those intricate creations, wondering which one he would pick— her sunburned ponytail hanging in the way, as usual. She could smell the faint remainder of spicy aftershave, mixed with the grassy scent of fish and the smell of sun-warmed tobacco. He selected a Royal Coachman, saying, "Well, Mother, I hope this will look like fish food instead of bird food." And then, perhaps because she hadn't soared away on the wings of another fantasy, he looked at Shelly and said, "Want to try a cast or two, Squirt?"

She squinted at Blaze, the oafish slug. His gray lower lip drooped as he dozed, shreds of grass and saliva drying on his bit. Surely other, nobler steeds would earn her favor on future days of whimsy. Dismissing him from importance for the moment, she watched as her Dad tied the Coachman quickly, with arcane knots, onto his leader. Its bright colors flashed in the sun, full of fire and unknowable results. Royal flies. Magic knots. And who knew what cryptic mysteries dwelt in the brains of fish? She glanced at her Mom, so ladylike in her pedal pushers and long red nails, her creel no doubt holding the seed of their main course for tonight. Her Mom tipped her curly head, grinned, and reached for Blaze's reins.

"Sure," Shelly answered. "It doesn't look too hard."

Closing her notepad, Shelly decided she wouldn't bother Skip with her Imperative scrawlings, runes from her silly imagination. She drifted into the kitchen, wondered idly if an evening thunderstorm might blank out the power before their lemon pepper chicken finished baking. Skip would pull into the driveway soon. She smiled.

The Bonefish Imperative: Dream On

"What happened? Did we lose the Easter Bunny? No, not Santa!" Shelly reached for an air of lightness. She puckered.

Skip dragged his heat-exhausted ass through the front door. "Nothing happened, just hating life." His eyes brightened a few degrees as he brushed her lips, like a match struck in a dark room. "Guys started off kinda slow, blew their only shots at tails this morning."

Shelly nodded. "They never seem to get it, do they, that each chance may be their last."

Leaning rods against the wall, Skip took his pliers out of their sheath and sank into the couch. He felt lower than whale shit. "Yeah, just like life. You buying?"

"On my way. So, pretty hot today. . . ." She opened the fridge, returned with two cold ones. The carbonation made a frosty pop. She handed Skip the refreshing fluid, *to quench his crumpled spirit.* She knew that this time of year the bonefish would leave the flats around midday, when the water could poach an egg. Then Skip would hunt for them out deeper. Not so exciting as casting to tails, but easier for his anglers to score.

Clients seldom factored in the degree of buck fever they would undergo when they finally set a big hairy eyeball on their target fish. Adrenaline shot through their veins like lightning when bonefish tails twinkled in the sun. Turned their legs to jelly. The sight also scrambled all their once well-coordinated casting signals from brain to elbow. Lot of guys could lay a fly on a dime—until they saw fish.

Skip sighed. "Mmmhmm. We went on out to four feet or so, those house muds. They had more than they could handle for a while. Not big fish, but we ended up four for seven." He pulled on his beer, his knuckles rimed with bonefish tracks.

"Great! That's really good! Then why do you seem terminally bummed?"

"Heat takes it out of you." He sipped, paused. Started again. "Maybe it was only one of those personality conflicts. Had the one really nice guy, not much of an angler, but he listened, trying to learn. I pointed out that his happy feet would end up standing on his fly line when he went to cast, if he didn't hold them still. He laughed, and really tried to fasten down his shoes after that. His pal, though. You could sharpen tools on his attitude. He already knew everything, been everywhere, friends with everybody. Or so he says. You know the kind, never heard a name he couldn't drop. But that didn't help his casting any. I tried to help him with his double haul, to gain him some much-needed distance, and I'd hear, 'Well, when I talked to McFamous at the school . . . ', or, 'I just read in an article that distance doesn't matter . . . ', or, 'That's not how we do it in. . . .' If he could get the fly line out of the damn boat, or even tie his own knots, I wouldn't have said a word. And

I don't care how they do it in Buttville. But hell, who cares, another day, another dollar."

Shelly frowned. Skip sounded burned as his mother's toast. "It's not so rare, some client who's a little too full of himself, right?" She made an effort to tease more out of him. Let him vent.

"Yeah, another day with a water balloon. Given a choice of being forced to hang with him the rest of my life, or eat a gun, I'd say pass the salt and pepper. Well, hell, let's go clean her up."

Outside, soaping the inside of the boat—Shelly lent a hand whenever possible, so they could enjoy more downtime together—she tried again to determine the source of this mood. Surely not this routine stuff—these little snags he laughed off most of the time. The fascinating mix of humanity he took fishing actually provided quite a few hilarious moments in their lives. She went for the gold, pressed the war button. "Get run over much today?"

A string of colorful epithets ensued. "There I am poling across Airport, and you know how big that flat is, when here comes an asshole who either doesn't know that those buoys out there mean No Motorized Vessels, or doesn't give a rat's ass. And of course, he cuts me off bigger than shit while I'm waving and hollering, giving him the Keys salute. Jeezus! And do you think there's a water cop within a hundred miles when you need one? No way. But just watch one come over the horizon if I crank up and go after some jet ski that slimed me."

Aha. There it is. "Remember when we hardly ever saw any other boats on the flats?" The wistful tone crept in unbidden.

"Yeah. Those days are history." Pessimism filled his voice.

Skip hosed off the boat while Shelly emptied the cooler, lugging trash to the can, sorting recyclables. Even though a good breeze had blown all day long, it had calmed enough now to let the sand flies drill holes into her skin with their horror-movie, acid-dripping jaws. At least out here in the sun the mosquitoes didn't add her to their meat menu. With no hint of wind, rivulets of sweat streaked down her legs, down her face, stinging into her eyes. *Aah yes, pure sex.*

Back inside their cool refuge she set dinner in the oven, said, "Want me to pull one? The world will be a happier place if I get in the shower."

"I'd be grateful."

Skip clicked on the tube to check out the weather conjecture, hoping for a radar shot or a satellite view. A lot of thunderheads around this afternoon. Damn forecasters would get all lathered up about some sexy system a thousand miles away, and, too wild-eyed to bother with their local weather, let vicious thunder cells come caterwauling down on unsuspecting mariners.

He swallowed a gulp of beer and listened to the drum of the shower spray steam up the hall. He knew he ought to go back outside and fix the snapped-off handle on the cooler—how *did* these guys break it?—but didn't move. Was the high he had long derived from guiding starting to fade? Not that he could tell, so more likely his vague discontent had some hidden source. Maybe he was coming down with something—he did kinda feel like the core of his body could replace the fuel rods in a nuclear reactor. True, occasionally the fight to jockey enough elbow room to put your clients on fish, that could suck butt loads. He had always believed fly-fishing should impart some form of communion with nature. Serenity and all that. Now and then, though, he'd bump into one of those strange days when it seemed like someone musta ran an ad in the paper, offering to give away money to the first five skiffs to reach the flats. Then, the only communion he knew came at the top of his voice, cussing at the latest idiot to crowd him. Of course, that activity provided its own brand of stimulation, nothing like the kick of a good conflict. A friend of his had controlled a recent clash admirably. Gunsel wanted to crowd so close to his spot he could goddam play pattycake. Then the gunsel turned all pissy when he got outmaneuvered, so his buddy just hollered over at him, "Okay, pal, we don't want to embarrass you (Skip really admired *that* insult) in front of your clients, so how about meet me at Generic Marina, around three, and we'll handle it then." Of course, the chicken shit never showed up. All swagger and no punch.

Some of the biggest Pains In the Butt lately were certain new guides. Amateurs so pathetically inept that they wouldn't get their business cards back from the printer before they starved out and went belly up. These guys, who hadn't guided long enough to suffer a centimeter of sun damage, would actually wear face masks, those balaclavas. A pal of his, he'd damn sure shoved a boat around for a ton of years, used one sometimes—born with that pinky skin, needed to cover up. But these PIBs just wanted to Assume the Look. As if they'd spent years outdoors instead of the ten minutes they toddled outside and practiced their seamanship lessons. They'd show up at the docks all decked out in these *costumes*—those goddam sweat-inducing "guide" shirts, strip tease breakaway pants, masks, bandannas, foreign legion hats, what next, ballerina slippers? Probably thinking that if they looked like *their* idea of a guide, all else would follow. *Well, we got their look hanging.*

Thank god the bloom of a fresh mud still jumped his heart rate. And those rare times when a tarpon rose to the top for his angler's fly, looking like a trout on steroids— yeah. He welcomed that punch of energy, those force waves of nervousness radiating off his anglers when they spotted a daisy chain of tarpon. You could power a whole goddam city on the tension from their sphincters. Sucking it up. Damn right.

The challenge to find the meandering waterways of tarpon, the secret haunts of permit, bonefish restaurants. To learn their ways made a life's work. Made his life work. How to fool them. Sometimes.

He often marveled at how fish could recognize they were being stalked. How one bonefish would spook, then hunt up its friends and spook them; how they could feel you coming no matter how silent your approach. Maybe the body of the skiff displacing water caused it. Like a big predator. Or maybe they sensed the energy from his intense stare. Funny how poor casters always wanted to wait until the boat pushed close to make their try, because by then the bones had sped up, aware of the need to feel nervous.

A doubt niggled, clattered on the edge of his perception. Another guide he knew, the guy admittedly given to paranoid prognostications, had recently infected Skip's thoughts with his dismal views. What if all the jet skis with their growls of acceleration, the dive boats throwing wakes big enough to surf, and yeah, the windsurfers, the kayakers, the waders and swimmers and rental boat snorkelers, Ma and Pa Kettle in their jon boat putt-putting along and trolling for barracuda on the buoyed off flats ("What buoy? We din't see no buoy"), and even all the Guide-in-Training PIBs and their ignorant ways—what if all this hubbub gave the bonefish indigestion? Maybe they would decide they no longer wanted to do lunch in Times Square.

Aw, hell, what kind of nutcake had he been eating? Every time he and Shelly scrimped up some bucks and tripped off to the newest rumored red hot destination, the fishing here still made him want to hurry home. He'd end up grousing during their whole stay, wondering why they had bothered to trek all over hell and gone when he enjoyed better fishing than this in his own damn backyard. He decided that he shouldn't let his imagination borrow trouble from a future that wouldn't arrive.

Cheering slightly, Skip emptied his beer and let his thoughts open onto a couple really fun days from last year. The weather gods had bestowed upon them a vigorous wind, severely limiting where he could hunt tarpon. He knew the backcountry would look like chocolate milk, and with white caps, hell, surfable waves, be too rough to negotiate. Most spots on the ocean side would throw thick swells at them, tall enough to swamp his skiff. Praying for a token from the fish deities, some counter-omen from an oceanic Valhalla, he picked his spot thinking, *It'll have to be right here, live or die.*

Beneficence fell from the skies, mostly in the form of spray in their teeth, but one of his anglers hooked up. Fairly early in the day, too—8:45 Skip noted, marking the time and tide for future reference. That happy client suddenly knew the joy rained down from a tower of tarpon. Photos, laughter. Aching back. His fishing buddy, however, couldn't make it happen. His turns on the bow that day yielded only whiffs, those tantalizing, maddening also-rans of tarpon fishing. In the roiling water he'd miss spotting the fish, even though Skip reminded him that he should cast with the same confidence whether *he* saw the tarpon or not. Skip worried. This guy *needed* a fish.

The wind hadn't improved its shitbird attitude much the next morning, so they elected to gamble their wad on the same spot. It had worked out well enough the day before, no capsizes, had some bites, even caught a nice one. But stress chewed into Skip's nerve endings. A few tarpon began to move through; shots were missed. The unanointed angler took the bow. Skip glanced at his watch and resolved to tune him up, "Okay, Buddy, it's almost 8:45 now, so it's not only your turn, hell, it's your *duty*, to catch a tarpon. And you'd better get it done On Time! Here they come, look at that string! Now get your ass ready! I want to see one of these jumbo mullet in the air!"

And damned if Buddy didn't do just that!

Memories like that, days like that, kept his heart pumping. Kept him getting up at five, earlier, seeking to share this awesome experience with another hopeful angler. That extraordinary moment when they flash—I'm linked to a fish whose ancestry traces back a hundred million years.

Good times. He recalled the roars of laughter that afternoon when a client had shattered his fly rod on a huge tarpon. That fish had *smoked* him. His angler had jacked on this colossal fish and, annoyed, it had jacked back. While Jacked-on-Fish gripped the rod butt and reeled like his entire portfolio hung on the hook, his buddy grabbed the newly-created tip section and struggled to maintain control. Chaos, with a shot of mirth. Shaken, not stirred.

Skip realized that he didn't know what he would do with his life, if not guiding, anyway. Still, he remembered the old fart he had seen tooling down the bicycle path along the highway a while back. Rusted and rickety bicycle, it pulled a little wagon. The wagon held the old fart's brown and white dog, a faded bundle of clothes, a spare bike tire. Skip had shuddered and thought at the time, *Probably a retired guide.* The phone rang, interrupting his reverie. Shit. He didn't feel like talking to anyone.

It was another guide. "What was that again?" Skip turned down the TV to listen. After he hung up, he thought, well, hell, why not? Can't hurt to take a look.

When Shelly reappeared, toweled pink and smelling like shampoo, he said, "Hey, want to take a trip?"

She smiled her mega-watt smile; she liked to travel. *This would be easy.*

"Sure. Where?"

"Some dinky-ass island, guess it's about halfway to nowhere."

"When?"

See how easy? "I don't know, need to make some arrangements, then we'll go take a look at this place, first chance."

An odd flicker crossed her face. *The Bonefish Imperative . . . but I never showed that silly thing to him. . . .* An infinite pool deepened in her gaze.

Hmmm, she's getting that strange expression. He hurried on, "Apparently they've got a resort or something on it—"

"Do you believe in synchronicity?" Shelly broke in.

Skip blinked, puzzled, "What? Oh, yeah, sure," then continued, "and they need someone who can find where their bonefish live." The first tumble of anticipation tossed in his stomach as he pictured miles of glistening blue-green flats. Hotel Bonefish. And, just maybe, not another boat in sight.

FIFTEEN

Swimming with Pete

Palm fronds slapped, the warm, soft air drooped with the scents of the Caribbean. Skip would never forget where he and Shelly had met Pete—one of the most romantic tropical settings imaginable. Water so blue it could break your heart, like Pete did Shelly's. But that hadn't been his fault, Pete had never intended to hurt anyone.

That she was already married didn't matter to Pete, or to Shelly, either. Skip guessed that he had taken the whole episode rather well, all things considered—at least the first part. But maybe that had something to do with Pete's placement in the natural order of things. You see, Pete belonged to the family of fishes, although a noble fish—a permit.

Shelly and he had packed up a duffle bag of clothes, fly-tying oddments, and armloads of fishing tackle and moved themselves with the lot to a remote Caribbean atoll. This, in order to manage a fishing camp that catered to fly anglers who sought to catch bonefish. Blinded by their enthusiasm for the magnificent surroundings, they gamely settled into a tiny cabin with a shared bath. Lacking any air conditioning but the sea breeze, they wasted no time installing screens, to help slow the nightly assaults of sand flies and mosquitoes. A water heater in all the bathrooms came next, these but two of their initial efforts in what they came to know as an always uphill battle. The owners wanted them to transform this drifting-toward-ramshackle lodge into a more upscale property, tune the guides up, position it more into step with the growing sophistication of traveling fly-fishers. If only they had provided a magic wand.

Equipment disasters became one point of reference by which they kept time: Shelly would say, "Yes, you remember, that was the day the cold drink cooler froze everything, and all the bottles broke, then dripped their syrupy frost all over the floor." Skip would counter, "Right, the week after I redlined our fastest boat thirty miles to the mainland to drag Scurvy out of that dugout canoe under some hellhole house where he had passed out from a three day drunk, and hauled his worthless butt back here so he could fix the goddam generator."

Another reference point, the repetitive spates of personnel discontent: "Did that happen after the guides threatened to quit if we asked them to stay out all day fishing, rather than come back to the lodge for lunch?" *The lazy assed prima donnas had decided that they needed their little nap and a hot lunch. And to sneak a few doobies of that square grouper they kept denying they had hidden somewhere in the bunkhouse. Not a one of them would make a decent pimple on a Keys guide's butt.*

Good things popped up now and then, too, though. Like that blustery night just days before the scheduled season opening. Since the whole staff had arrived, Skip figured a little socializing would benefit all, and broke out a deck of cards. None knew any card games, so he tried to teach them poker. Figuring that the rules for 21 should prove easy enough to describe, he began explaining the different values, face cards and such. He plowed headfirst into a road block when he discovered that the crew held but a dim comprehension of the symbols. Backtracking, he and Shelly explained, at length. Finally, they managed a few hands of the most outrageous version of 21 they had ever played. Talk about laugh your asses off, the smiles lit up the dining room. Then the squalls increased their fury and all hands dashed to the dock. Soaked to the bone, they dragged the new skiffs onto the beach and lashed them to palm trees.

Their life established itself into a perpetual slog of seven twenty-fours. A grinding litany of ordering mechanical parts that wouldn't arrive for weeks and when they did, wouldn't fit. Of mediating childish disputes between self-pitying minds: "Jocko gots a bigger tip than me." *Yeah, maybe Jocko put his guy on fish for a change, numbnuts, instead of keeping them just twenty feet too far away like you always do.* Of twentieth century paperwork—government reports, licensing, payroll—with eighteenth century tools—"Has anyone seen the pencil?" *Thank god, by accident or foresight, they had packed Shelly's little solar calculator.* Generator mishaps, read breakdown, always happened at midnight. *Where is that Scurvy bastard, drunk again?* Scrambling for provisions and striving to foil the disappearance of same, while they dashed to the mainland for the next group of anglers, turned into a spirited contest. Question: *Where have all the coffee trays gone?* Answer: *Me ain't know.* And then came that weekly turnover of sparkly-eyed guests, who expected the best fishing vacation of their lives. Skip now realized that you could talk to anyone who has done a stint in the third world and you would hear much the same inventory of nearly incredible catastrophes. Never a dull moment, much less enough of them strung together to count as a decent night's sleep.

Skip also soon learned that attempting to hone the skills of these guides took more than just his experience and fly-fishing skill. At first the guides feared the poling platforms. Through a ticker tape storm of red tape they had finally managed to import new, Florida-style skiffs. *We fall off*, they complained. Insisting that the guides must rotate their flats to avoid chousing the same schools of bonefish every day—a waste of his air. The guides would simply agree, and then boogie on back to their habitual spots. Naturally, certain areas soon contained bonefish with a very sour outlook. He soon discovered that they had no knowledge of the tides, and no interest in learning its effect on the fishing. Even before season opening, Skip had challenged them to range a bit farther from camp, pole out new waters in search of productive flats. Following up on their performance of this task, Skip would find them lolling about at a nearby lobster shack, shooting the shit with their lobster fishing cousins. And poling? They preferred dumping their clients out on the flats, making them wade, so that then the guides only needed to walk along and point out the bonefish, not have to break into a pesky sweat by shoving that boat. *No shit, those are tails? Yeah, I really needed you here to show me that. Dammitall, but he got pissed at them sometimes.* But forget firing the worst of the worthless. Two walls blocked that happy solution. Number one, the labor laws of this nation required the same extensive documentation necessary to shitcan an American civil servant, a pain in the ass but not impossible. Number two, impossible; the owners, the same forked tongue folks who had promised Skip carte blanche in running the place, would set up a whine louder than an Indy race car." *But (*insert the interchangeable names of various shits-for-brains here*) has been with us for years, he's one of our best guides. Try talking to him.* Yeah, talk.

Shelly encountered her own hells. A cook who wouldn't, except when her spirit deemed it fitting. Dinner, sure, oh, say five-ish. Never mind that the guests couldn't possibly return from the flats at four and have the chance to rinse their gear, shower, and enjoy a sunset rum on the deck before their evening meal of her truly vile concoctions. After trying to gag down one dinner, Skip had remarked, "Goddam, Shelly, if I have to eat this shit I'd rather starve to death!" When asked to prepare different fare, and present those meals on schedule, the cook quit—and yammered unfair so stridently that she managed to drag the entire household staff off the island. Shelly thrilled, oh yes, to this opportunity to test exactly how many positions she could work at once, until the thank God replacements arrived midweek. The new cook, however, had dropped from some culinary heaven, and at least that aspect of their lives improved, with fried lobster, johnnycake, and key lime pies.

Still, when Skip couldn't endure one more autocratic demand that he appear at another national agency on behalf of the camp's owners, in order to explain away the faux pas of prior years, when one more thirty mile boat ride over open seas to that squalid town loomed, he could steal a few minutes of time out. Instead of eating his midday sandwich, he could cast to bonefish on the nearby flats. And when members of the household staff demonstrated their stubborn propensity for leaving well enough alone, where dirt was concerned, Shelly could slip into the tourmaline water off the dock and snorkel away from—or maybe toward—reality. The clownish paint jobs of queen triggerfish, their ability to dial their colors up and down like a rheostat as they negotiated the staghorn corals, simply knocked her swim fins off. Those stolen moments kept them both on speaking terms with sanity.

The camp dog, a chocolate Labrador named Sheila, accompanied Shelly on her swimming forays. Sheila's companionship apparently arose from her perceived need to protect Shelly, because she had lost her pal Ranger, the other camp dog, to the local saltwater crocodile. Skip and Shelly had watched this huge water lizard patrol silently by in the dark, hoping for foolish mammals, its eyes like red dot sights. Although this canine tragedy had happened the year before they arrived, the loss and the danger stayed fixed firmly in Sheila's doggy engrams, so every time Shelly stepped down the ladder at the end of the dock, she would bark like a madwoman. Warningly, pleadingly, frantically. And when Shelly still insisted on floating about with face mask and fins, *oh you oblivious human!* Sheila would plunge in to guard her, dogpaddling nearby— and sometimes rather uncomfortably right over the top of Shelly's back—with a very worried doggy face. What the sweet animal could have done if that leviathan ever did cruise by during the day is anyone's guess. She'd probably have served as dragon lunch, just like Shelly.

Anglers familiar with the saltwater game fish called permit, *trachinotus falcatus*, will likely find what follows difficult to comprehend. Permit have a well-earned notoriety as crafty and hard-to-approach, and they rank right at the top of the tough-to-hook fish pantheon, for a fly rodder. But Skip had finally come to believe that they possess a strong curiosity, along with their ability to disappear in a blink. That's what he thought now, but, of course, he didn't know exactly what to think about it then. All that either of them understood was that on one enchanted day Shelly had hovered over a coral head maybe a hundred feet from the dock. She watched a squirrel fish, so big eyed and crimson, flare its dorsal fin at her in prickly warning to stay away from its acreage. Then, with Sheila sploshing the sea into foam not three feet away, Shelly turned her gaze to another flank of the coral, seeking a new gaudy fish to admire. A permit materialized.

The permit watched her, rolling his large dark eyes and floating suspended in the water, effortlessly tracking along as Sheila and Shelly moved from coral head to sea fan. Shelly referred to it as He, not that they could tell, but for want of knowing they stuck with that gender appointment. He showed no fear, a tidbit of information that she eagerly relayed to Skip.

Skip had caught and released one of this permit's family members not two miles from the camp—this on the first day of their exploratory visit to the site—so he knew good numbers of them abounded. But he had developed a strong appreciation for the wariness of the species, so at first he thought Shelly had mistaken this fish with another of its carangid cousins, one with a similar sheen and shape. Vexed, she plopped the fish identification book from the lodge bookshelf right into his lap. "I've seen them before, you know. He's this one."

Catching a permit on fly counted as such a gala occasion, often resulting in a tip of fifty bucks U.S., that the guides would often take a crack at duping the guests. They would swear, *Fish be a permit!* when the guest had actually only landed another member of the jack family. This was just one of their chosen scams to gyp big tips out of the less witting guests. *Anything but earn it,* Skip grumbled.

Pete, Shelly gave him a name on their second outing, kept showing up. How did she know he was the same fish? How does someone tell one Doberman pinscher from another? It was Pete. He hung around close enough, though just out of arm's reach, for her to carefully study his iridescent silvery form, the sapphire sheen across his back, the contour of that buttery streak on his belly. He seemed entertained, perhaps by the contrast between her passive observations and Sheila's eggbeater legs. He would follow them along as they checked on the welfare of graceful angelfish, or smiled at baby rays the size of pancakes. He carried an aloofness, an aura of distinction. In his milieu there lived the reef fish, rainbow decked, amusing creatures; the apex predators like sharks, to avoid; the guileless brown canid, certainly no danger; the slow pink human, evidently intriguing; and himself—radiant, different from all.

One day Skip walked out on the dock with his fly rod in hand, intending to steal a lunch break bonefish cast or two. By then he had witnessed, from his perspective on the dock, that sickle fin and shadow of light as it toodled along with Sheila and Shelly. *Damnedest thing I ever saw,* he had mused, watching the unlike buddies enjoy their aimless companionship. Shelly waved to him from the water, and guessed, correctly, that Skip had decided to find out what transpired when he threw a fly toward this chummy fish. Quite a bit has been written about how fish can see out of the water, and how far. It still seemed almost prescient, though, the way Pete vanished as soon as Skip started casting.

That whole incident made Shelly ill at ease, as if torn between Skip's happiness and the contentment of this docile permit. She didn't want Pete's innocent meanderings with her spoiled. Nor did she want Skip to suffer disappointment. Skip took her hint, though, in a good-natured way. He admitted that maybe Pete had grown a trifle too savvy for him, hanging out as he had with her crowd, and it might work out better for all concerned to just let him serve as the saltwater icon he had become. Instead of saying, "Gee, Shell, don't you think you're getting a little silly over swimming around with this damn fish?" He understood, all too well, that they each had sparse enough moments of wonder in this dream job turned nightmare. Why tamper with those few fantasies they had found for escape?

In the fresh crop of guests that they picked up at the airport every weekend, this new group differed little from the others, really, except that it contained a man who owned a well-known fly shop on very famous trout waters. Skip and Shelly had not enjoyed the chance to fish in those hallowed waters. That treat remained an item still on their to-do list, so they eagerly absorbed what they could learn about the river from this man.

Big trout, they heard, and trout that must put notches on their fins, judging by the number of flies they snipped from the leaders of hapless anglers. Catch and release, of course, so even when these trout suffered an error in judgement, they were spared to provide recreation, in all senses of the word, for another day. Ah yes, Skip and Shelly dreamed, someday we'll stride quietly down the turf-padded edges of these famous streams and meet these trout, trout maybe even with names. Like Pete.

For the time being, though, Skip and Shelly knew they must wring every possible delight from their term in the tropics. Despite the reality that sleep had become a mere blink between days so long they felt like weeks, they found things to love. They tried catching the big super-male parrot fish who surfed on wavelets that lapped the reef, a mere hundred yards away. Those stocky bronze-red, neon-green garish fish snubbed their flies but delighted their eyes. They caught countless weenie bonefish, pale as icicles but fast as light. They treasured those tranquil moments before the bustle of evening enveloped them, sipping an icy beer on the lodge deck. The waning sun would make a mango wash of the sky on one side while the moon lifted, a pale melon slice, on the other. They liked hearing the haunting melodies that echoed under the palms, smoky reggae expanding through the balmy day, emanating from the carpenter's tape player as he undertook repairs. Rasta Skip and Rasta Shelly he called them, his gold tooth flashing. They played with Sheila, kept her free of ticks and shiny, and regularly observed their other new buddy, part of their world by then, Pete.

Well before breakfast one morning Shelly began work in the cubbyhole office. Untangling the Byzantine requirements of that country's still very foreign social security setup, she slammed several mugs of caffeine in an attempt to shock herself smart. The cook and her helper fried bacon in the next room, secure in their knowledge that, unlike previous years, their contributions would be tendered. Movement caught Shelly's eye, and she glanced through the opened shutter. A few of the guests had begun straggling up the conch shell-lined path toward the lodge from their cabins, a couple hundred yards away. The car dealer and his wife, two guys from New England, the fly shop man. He carried something in addition to the strung rods the others held. She should have pulled her eyes away. A layer of vibrating bee wings covered her skin. She stared at him as he neared. She *needed* to look away. But something heavy, larger than the lodge, held her to the wooden chair. Her interior twisted. Pete.

Later, after Shelly trudged back to the lodge, back from their room, back from their loss, she found Skip sitting on the deck. The guests had all disappeared over the horizon on their skiffs with their guides. Skip just sat there, his face blanched, like when rage drives all the blood to your heart. Shelly's heart held blood, too.

"The asshole says, 'Hey, we can have this for dinner'," Skip's voice had that low, quiet Dirty Harry menace.

"No way," Shelly choked over the painful rock in her throat.

"No shit."

Skip carried Pete's towel-wrapped body down to the dock, with Sheila and Shelly tagging behind. Sheila sensed the mood, too. She didn't even bark when Skip and Shelly stepped into the old wooden camp panga and fired the outboard. They puttered slowly out toward the reef line, through the cut, and into water clear as insight. While Skip fashioned a tether to a massive concrete block, Shelly held Pete, no longer lit from within. She looked at his once soft eyes, now glazed. She ran the tips of her fingers gently over his skin, which felt like the inside of her arm. Finally Skip created a harness with magic knots and attached Pete to his marker stone. They said good-bye and returned him to his element.

Going in, they discussed the strange and bitter ways of people. How they could expound on one ethic at home and display another when out of sight of their neighbors. They wondered how Mr. Fly Shop would feel if they marched into his store with one of his revered brown trout hanging stiff and lifeless from a stringer. But they knew they wouldn't have the heart to take revenge by punishing a blameless animal—it would be akin to coldly snuffing his pet dog. Like what he had done to Pete.

SIXTEEN

Amazing Days

Skip's energy soared. Smoked turkey breast coursed through his blood, fueled the thrust of his graphite push-pole, powered his hunt for bonefish across Keys flats as clear and blue as mouthwash. Jerry, his angler today, had thankfully called a lunch break.

Occasionally his clients would indulge in tag team lunching. Like that day when the amply sized chocolate lover had homesteaded the cooler-lid seat all morning. Skip's thoughts skittered a moment; could there exist some universal rule demanding that the bulkiest angler invariably select *that* seat, thereby buckling the top? This individual had broken fast on candy bars the size of a tarpon leader stretch box, washing them down with a diet (of course) cola, while the other fly rodder manned the casting deck. Then they quickly swapped positions. As a result Skip couldn't access his sandwich unless he broke into the rhythm of the fishing cycle, never a productive option for a guide. Rather starve than miss a shot at a fish.

Quick, witty, and willing to lunch, Jerry had also shown a gift for comic declarations. He would suddenly bubble over with what Skip considered the most amazing comments, like, "I'm not the Jerry that jerry-built." Naturally, Skip would set off pondering who *that* "Jerry" had been, and why he'd done such rotten work that every slapped together, mismatched, warped-boarded, bent-nailed project wore his name. And then, staying on the subject of mythical names, Jerry pipes up with, "What kinda name ya think is Bo Peep?"

Skip chuckled. "Hey, I'm only a fly-fishing guide, you know, entomology, not etymology." Not that flats guides had to worry overmuch about mayfly hatches.

Jerry's quirky humor sure added to the fun of the fishing day. Way different than a guy he had guided only last week, who—just ask him—had discovered the ocean and invented hooks. Actually, every saltwater thought in his head came from a group of easily recognized sources, but he seemed to be one of those, "When I want your opinion, I'll give it to youse," gentlemen. Hard to teach people who already know it all. Now that Skip surveyed his memory a bit, he'd damn sure fished his share of clients worthy of their own television docudrama. Something about the nature of the bidness, he supposed, just the troubled fruits of an exotic life—or the flipside.

He'd never forget the Hitler eyelash charter. His folks that day, a nice lady and her husband, had booked a spin-fishing trip for bonefish. They were truly pleasant people who wore their obvious mileage well. But, bless her, every time the lady turned around, "they" obtruded: black, laterally abbreviated like the famous despot's mustache, out to there, and fake as a starlet's chest measurement. Skip had furtively checked the date on his watch—nope, not the last of October. *Scratch the costume party.*

Neither could he overlook the two guys who pro-claimed that they had long hankered for a beer, um, bone-fishing trip. The one who stood tall and beefy kept clapping his hands together twice, hard, announcing, "Because I'm (clap, clap) PUMPED UP!" The other guy, a tower of pallor, guffawed at every repetition. It *was* pretty damn funny, and became even more so as the day progressed. These two had jammed the ice chest with at least a full case of beer, and when Skip commented that no room remained for their lunch, Pump had boomed, "Hell, that IS lunch!"

So off they trekked to enjoy a sunny, salty morning on the grassy flats. Continuous mirth had ruled the day in the style of banter and red-ass, them slamming beers, Skip fu-tilely remarking the presence of bonefish, at which neither Pump nor Tower bothered fixing their attention. At noon they sped to a marina to refill the ice chest—with more beer. By 2:30 Pump declared himself, "Ten feet tall and bulletproof! Because I'm (clap, clap) PUMPED UP!"

Keep those bonefish keyed to the hottest news flash, Skip thought. *A powerful racket makes them ravenous, oh yeah.* By afternoon back at the dock, Pump remained festive, Tower looked like a sun-dried tomato, and both said they had dire need of, yep, More Beer. They didn't even appear to have caught too much of well, anything, but to Skip's notion they really ought to have copped quite a buzz. Capacity? These guys could shame a whole frat house.

Skip's energy had leveled off a bit by now, but he felt damn good. The sun baked his shoulders, and now he sensed a seaweed essence in the air. Maybe bonefish ahead. Jerry had it going, rod ready, eyes peering into the water.

"Jerry, cast one at ten thirty, about forty feet, see 'em there?" Unreal. Skip squinted hard. Sure enough, long graceful side stripe and those lemon yellow fins—snook on the oceanside bonefish flats! "Good, good, no! Quick! Cast again! Ten feet to the left!" Damn. Oh well, nobody would believe it if they caught one anyway. "Nice try, they just slid on by without looking. Never seen them here before."

"Seen what?"

"Snook." Skip shook his head. Life kept turning out more and more amazing, and so did the fishing, which amounted to the same subject.

Jerry laughed. "National Lampoon Goes Bonefishing, right?"

"No shit, man, honest, those really *were* snook." *Hell, Jerry didn't buy it and he was right here.*

He poled onward, thinking he dared not omit from this fascinating array the young, earnest trout fisherman on his first tarpon trip to The Keys. Skip had spent the entire evening prior tying up the elaborate tarpon leaders, Bimini twists, shock tippets, multiple knots. At the end of the day, Earnest, handing Skip back his Buchanan Special that polite way anglers do with borrowed flies on trout streams, out of habit, bit the fly clean off the leader, quick as a beaver. Skip looked at the leader, now too short to tie on another fly. Wound it up and threw it away in his cooler. *Ruined.*

Another of his tarpon anglers Skip had come to regard as Mr. Fastidious. Although a favored client, his remarkably precise habits had led to him squander one of the scant good head-on shots of a brutal day. The wind howled from the east, slapped them, coating faces, bodies, the inside of the boat with salt spray. *Ahhh, yes, I'm living the dream,* Skip thought. Scudding clouds frequently blocked visibility, notching up the difficulty, so decent shots had been scarce as honesty in politics. A few singles, a double—overall, piss poor, uphill, and into the wind. Finally, a superb fish approached. Pine green dorsal easy to see, swimming near the top of the water column, happy, riding high down the Tarpon Trail. Skip's heart raced, he called, "Here she comes, get ready!"

Mr. Fastidious, serenely nibbling on his luncheon, rewrapped his sandwich with care, opened the cooler with great caution so as not to make a sound, and placed his food inside. He prudently placed his drink inside, too, so it would not spill, and closed the lid without the slightest thud. He neatly wiped his fingertips, so as not to soil the cork on his fly rod. And then, at last, he picked up his rod to make a cast to the majestic creature, who had by now reached the nine o'clock position—the perfect place for them to see eye to eye. A crossing shot. You find better odds in Las Vegas.

One otherwise normal charter consisted of two fellows who he had come to think of as the Jacket Twins, Coats and Cloaks. Because every time the boat moved to a new location, they splayed themselves flat onto the deck of the skiff with their coats jerked over their heads, as if the wind might blow their minds. He remembered, too, with a smile, that unfortunate soul who wound up with the pink zebra sunburn stripes, caused by applying his sunscreen on the boat, unevenly. No pesky sunburn in store for the Mummy, however, the solar averse lady who had swaddled herself head to foot in towels while her husband fished. He had always kind of liked that movie.

Brought to mind that morning his client showed up wearing the same black soled shoes from the day before. Damn things looked like hiking boots. Came to boat cleaning hour after their first extra-long, soupy hot day, and Skip had needed to spend an added full thirty minutes with a scrub brush and compound wax, removing marks from the deck. The whole time thinking, *It doesn't get any worse than this.* So he told Black Soles, "We got a problem with those shoes." Soles said, "I brought a towel to stand on." As if he'd remain firmly planted when he hooked a fish. Skip handed him his pocket knife and a spool of monofilament, and thus Black Soles came to fashion booties for his feet. His mummy apparel ignited considerable amusement from other guides back at the dock, adding to the legend.

A certain wife, enduring her private edition of The Vacation from Hell, sat cross-legged on the deck and slapped down defiant games of solitaire while her hubby cast to impressive schools of bonefish. Even when several shimmery, canny permit floated by to zap Skip's composure and adrenalize her groom, she deigned no notice. A popsicle of resolve to blot this conscription from her life. *Enjoying that Nature experience, yeah.*

"Jerry, point your rod! Left, left, there." A skirmish line of bones marched, well, finned, toward the skiff. "Put one on 'em! Perfect, good, strip it, good."

The shallow window of low tide through which bonefish see the fly also forms a shallow window of heightened awareness and safety concerns. They fear not only sharks and larger, bullyboy fish, but also rampaging, fish-eating birds. So imagine their concern when. . . .

Three F-16s screamed low in tight formation. Hot rod, top gun types cremating hundred dollar bills, flashing in the sun, waggling proud insignia: let's Buzz that bonefish flat and show those slow-moving lowly citizens the true power of Manly men.

Terrified fish scattered like shot from an open choke, and about that fast.

Jerry stared heavenward, stunned out of his reflex silliness.

Skip felt a brief burst of anger, swelling with the speed of a whacked shinbone. He shoved his pushpole against the limestone bottom, spun the skiff, and struck a transverse course to the edge of the flat. He tasted salt as droplets of sweat trickled south.

Poling along, he tried to think more about his extraordinary clients and less about the uncivil disruption. Those jet jerks came so close that if they hadn't been wearing masks he could have judged the closeness of their shaves. He sighed, and then, sent into negative space by the sonic insult, recalled the yuppie couple who had bickered without end, snapping zingers that Skip believed most spouses only mouthed after they had retained separate attorneys. An expense of quality time. He had broken into their chinking to call out, "Bonefish! Hurry!" in an effort to get them to cast something other than aspersions. Such efforts usually earned him the look a wasp displays on sting patrol. By couch time that night he ached like he had weathered a train wreck. Talk about bad soap opera—it took extra shampoo to wash the bitterness of them out of his head.

Not many of his fishing trips turned out off kilter that way. But plenty of them were rife with, um, color. Like the day a woman showed up with her husband for a bonefish quest wearing her Walkman and high heels. On a skiff? That put him in mind of the dude (he decided that if you do this you definitely rank as a dude of some sort) who had deck soles put on his alligator cowboy boots.

Talking about cool outfits, the Velcro Guys had girded their loins like knights of olde, donning back braces with magnets, casting wristbands that fastened to their rods, elbow braces with magnets, and who knows where and what else. They looked like a couple of bonefish gladiators. One even changed his hat and sunglasses at noon. You've got your morning hat and your midday hat, don't ya know, and those daybreak sunglasses just won't do under the noonday sun. And on the subject of hilarious, if you wanted to see a funny look on two faces you should have been a pelican floating by his skiff that day the guy took a whizz in Skip's just-emptied beverage jug. No malice intended, he simply had no inkling that to pinch some pennies a guide might re-fill the jugs.

In all fairness, though, he supposed that fishing guides accounted for just as many quirky behaviors as their clients. Almost as superstitious as baseball players, many captains dreamed up arcane rules and rituals to keep the jinx of a fishless day from visiting their boats. For instance, everyone in south Florida knew about the famous offshore captain who banned anything reminiscent of one particular tropical fruit from his charters. Skip had even heard that one day he had returned to the dock so his clients could offload an offending bottle of sunscreen that displayed the taboo *word* on its label. Another guide had become famous among his peers for (warning, the following phrases are rated "R") laying pipe. This term used here in reference to performing a gross bodily function, normally dealt with in the john, off the back of his poling platform. Skip suspected that maybe if the EPA could curb this guy, any near-shore water quality problems in the Keys would disappear.

"We'll look out here," Skip told Jerry when they reached the deeper water. "Those freaked out fish'll avoid the shallows for a while."

"What do I watch for here?" Jerry said, examining the bottle-green water.

"Puffs of mud, where they're feeding. We'll catch you one; these fish can't see us as well."

And they did. A chubby member of the bonefish circus, with its three-ringed eyes and bubble gum lips. Jerry went bozo with glee.

Shelly flip-flopped down the stairs to greet him as Skip backed the boat trailer into their coral rock driveway.

"Another amazing day," Skip muttered, reaching gratefully for the ice-cold beer in her outstretched hand.

"You hear all that noise?" She squinched her sun blushed forehead. "Those jets?"

Skip puzzled over why she mentioned it, then realized that the planes had probably rumbled just yards over their deck, and not three seconds after they had spooked Jerry's fish. He hoped she hadn't been out there in her bikini—but they would have torched by too fast. Anyway, not too much noisy ever happens in the Keys, well, except when the sirens blared down Useless One on the way to scrape up tourists who have smashed into each other. A relatively frequent event, it usually transpired as a result of the participants gaping at the lucent sea rather than avoiding that boring rental car in front of them. Oh yeah, the mosquito planes made quite a roar when they swooped mere feet over treetops and power lines to release the mists that killed the tiny vampires. The big vintage bombers often terrorized tourists who thought the Keys were being attacked, but the spraying saved them all from a fate worse than bit.

"Hear them?" he grinned. "Those reckless little pricks boogered our fish. We bad vibed the hell out of 'em."

"Karma."

"Say what?"

"I guess that'll teach them to scare your fish."

Still puzzled, Skip sluiced beer down his parched throat and waited for the punch line.

Shelly obliged. "They wing clipped each other, one guy had to eject before his plane crashed."

Skip popped goosebumps. *Some days you get the magic, others, a curse—but it's always amazing.*

SEVENTEEN

Howling under the Tarpon Moon

"Come on man, can ya stay just a little longer? I'm sure the tarpon will hit those sea fans," Kirby pleaded, "any minute now." His grizzled ponytail hung limp, his fly rod gestured over glossy flats.

Skip shrugged. June, and the steamy Florida Keys atmosphere had frazzled them both, so he felt about ready to pack it in. He hadn't intended to make quite such a marathon of it, yet he had savored this scheduled Guide's Day Off. He probably should have chilled at home, rested up for his next spate of charters, but he still desperately craved what his wife Shelly would call an "ionic bond" with a tarpon. She would say something like, "To breathe its spindrift breath." Hell, he really just wanted to touch one of these goddam overgrown herring.

A depressing string of his days lately had gone to helplessly watching his anglers blow perfect shots and bumble away eager bites—yet not actually *catch* a single one of these Goliaths. Like most guides, he generally derived his maximum kick from the simple acts of finding and tricking the quarry. After all, once you get the bite, all that pumping and reeling only delays your next chance to fool the next fish. But the zest of success had gone too long untasted. He ached, not only to see that dazzle of wet silver rip the air, but to also have one of these armored fish nudge right up to the boat. He needed to count coup.

Most of today the tarpon had shunned them—swimming fast, or deep, dragging their fins on the bottom, or swinging wide of the skiff. Acting like real dicks. Oh, he had managed to jump one, enjoyed a moment or two of that bone-softening rush that puts color in the vision of life—until the hook straightened out on a Long Distance Release. *Pretty damn typical when I fish with Kirby, this kind of luck.* He wished Shelly could have come along, her fey spirit might have altered the outcome.

Kirby, however, remained convinced that the tarpon had worm hatch on their minds. This fabled event occurs under strong moon tides during the tarpon migration. At some mystic moment palolo worms would come boiling out of their sponge and sea fan habitats and tarpon would snap and slurp at them like starved trout after *hexagenias.* For about the first thirty minutes, until the water so saturated with naturals it turned into palolo soup, you could drop a fly into seething tarpon and reasonably expect a hookup.

"Okay," Skip said. "Let's pole on over where the fans are a little thicker, see if any come through." *At least my face has quit melting, bad as one of those Sixties bathroom-mirror acid trips.*

The sea had glistened all afternoon with the lucent green of a beer bottle, *nor any drop to drink.* And the sun had burnt into them, hard as the yellow peach halves back in grade school cafeteria. Finally a huge anvil thunderhead emerged, spreading its influence from Everglades to ocean side flats. Thunder grumbled over mainland Florida. The cloud shadow deftly hammered the ambient degrees down to a bearable level, but now visibility sucked.

Skip kept bumming over his slump. He wondered if he could pin a little blame on the rising asshole consciousness of modern life, let progress take some heat for this recent decline in his catch ratio. Yeah, when clients nutted up and missed perfect head-on shots, it always provided Purina for a guide's nightmares. But what had ever happened to an angler's ability to yank a chunk of that inner fire, that *desire* from down deep, to *punch* a cast ten feet farther into the wind? He wanted to think that maybe the lack of serious consequences, for damn near anything, held a measure of the burden. Historically, if humans weenied out instead of hoisting the bucket from the well, they went dry. Or if they didn't put enough heart into sprinting those last twenty yards for the cave, they filled a sabertooth sandwich. Nowadays when human error took over, when we failed or goofed or even committed a crime, some rationalization expert on self-esteem would coach our whining—yes, all due to a very bad hair day, or some (largely bogus) childhood trauma, poor thing. Never, hey, ass face, You Fucked Up. Except maybe on a guide's boat. Skip couldn't understand how in the hell those esteem gurus figured you could build self-respect without accepting responsibility.

"Hey man, want a brewski?" Kirby popped a can to suck it dry with vacuum speed. One gulp. Awesome.

Skip planted the pushpole, looked around to check the sea fan acreage. "Naw, thanks, I'm driving. Hand me that orange stuff."

"Yeah, about here, somewhere," Kirby passed Skip's jug, wolfed another cold one, emitted a yeasty burp.

"It's not really that good a moon yet, though." Skip thought Kirby, driven by his own quirky motives, might have miscalculated.

"Oh man, there hasn't been much wind—they've gotta come."

Tarpon madness. This time of year everyone shared the power of schizophrenia.

The tarpon had an excuse, justification enough their budding courtships and consummations. And then those worms. In relative size to them like grapes to humans, the worms might as well be grapes dipped in mescaline. The argent giants would careen gaily from sea fan to sponge, gulping, slashing, popping, rolling. They would follow the tidal flow as the worms washed to sea, excited, rattling, and jostling like a flooded dumpster full of churning, bobbing bottles. With messages. The message: If your fly doesn't resemble these gourmet treat invertebrates, fuggedaboudit.

Fishing guides became so weirded out during these strange days—exhausted, confused, delirious—that they would call buddies to learn who among the lucky had found happy fish, and by the time the dialed phone began to ring, forget who they had called. A product, no doubt, of long, sweaty days and short, anxious nights. The quality of light meets the quantity of night.

While Kirby searched the water in front of the skiff, hoping for a fishy blur, a distant dorsal arching skyward, anything that connoted tarpon, Skip covered the rest of the picture. *Kind of an advantage, fishing with buds, because they hunt for fish, too.* His best clients helped as well, and it definitely compounded the hookup ratio. Three hundred sixty degrees times eight hours makes a lot of brine to study, especially when those same two eyes must also watch out for that Cockroach sizzling by their ears. Clients, bless 'em, really ought to come with a warning label.

Kirby sighed, "I don't know. I think maybe it's early yet."

"Yeah. Hey, did I tell you, the other day, I had pushed my guy around in ten feet of water since, felt like, the last Ice Age; definitely not worried about needing time at the gym, there's that. Well, damned if this guy didn't drop one right on the money, smack in line with a tarpon. And this fish, flaunting its tarpon mastery of the erratic, made this regal glide towards my guy's Black Death, delicately opened its maw, sipped it in, turned away. Heart-stopping, but so what else is new, right? Well, then that tarpon rolled, bottom-side up! *backward* over its head! Shelly called it a reverse dolphin, some trick she learned in water ballet. Yeah, that big Mamoo swooped upside down, then twisted back over as simple as we breathe."

"Cool."

"Major."

They continued their vigil. Waiting for tarpon to push allowed plenty of time to stare into green shimmer, to reflect. But where seers gazed into crystal balls or bowls of water to see future or past, Skip felt lucky if his gazing revealed the present. So much to monitor, out there on the flats; saltwater fishing required profound concentration. He had read some stuff about human perception, how the lag between event and cognition distanced our perception, limited it to fractions of reality. Oh sure, hard to miss big happenings, like spotted eagle rays catching air. Their wedgie bods—polka dotted cocoa, that white ghost-face underneath—would soar, kersplash! Or bottlenose dolphins, cheerful, breaching and splashing across shallows, sewing through waves. But the nuances came harder: the things that fish would tell you, and when to believe them.

Tarpon fax—like the belief that the lead fish never bites. Except for that one yesterday, swimming with such a flourish it had made Skip smile out loud. High in the water, flirting, digging it and the attentions of her suitors, a court clad in ardor. She bit. His client whiffed her.

Or like their "Oooh! What a *big* scary fly!" act, as a tarpon would turn itself inside out and silly with refusals on an Apte Too. The same fly that had caught a fish the day, maybe the hour before. And then the next *Megalops* that swam by would garbage it. . . .

It proved, at least to Skip's mind, that each tarpon took on an individual personality. After all, based on the study of growth rings in their otoliths, or ear bones, fish biologists had verified that these slow-maturing fish enjoy a long lifespan. A thirty-five year old tarpon had gained size enough to seriously put the hurts to you. He suspected that those bigger ones, the Mamoos that could snap off hundred-pound shock tippets like rotted cotton thread, had damn near reached retirement age. You'd naturally expect any animal that survives that long to acquire a distinct character and attitude. Get downright curmudgeonly.

Skip glanced at Kirby, stared hopelessly into the sea fans a while longer, then said, "A week or two back, my client, a great guy, super jazzed over his first tarpon trip, woke up suddenly and saw the lights shining outside around his motel. He thought, "It's daybreak!" He glanced at his watch, sideways in the dark. "Oh no! Six! I'm supposed to meet my guide at six!" He grabbed the phone and called. I answered, made that long crawl out of serious torpor, managed to mumble, "Morning, Grayson. Uh, you know what time it is?" Grayson checked his watch. Groaned. "A quarter to three."

"Were you pissed?"

"Nope, guy was just stoked. Made bedtime damn early that night, though. Speaking of bedtime, it's getting on, and I think we're doomed, man."

"Just a few more minutes, I *know* they're gonna get here," Kirby fretted. He popped another brewski and vacuumed it empty to assuage his anxiety.

Skip checked the thunderhead, the crummy light, his wristwatch, tried to ignore the pain in his feet burning all the way to his butt—*should have stayed home and held down the couch.* Sighed, said, "Here's another good one. Last week I guess, I had hurried to start extra early with my anglers, trying to nab that spot at the point. Finally got this new motor propped right and the speed about peeled their faces off, way cool. So we nailed our spot and the light still had that smoke gray look, but a few rollers came swimming along and we saw them well enough to get decent shots. But later on, nine or so, up putts some sponge-headed gunsel, thought he'd cut in front of us. He should know better, but he tried it anyway."

"An epidemic lately," Kirby agreed. "No courtesy left." He stretched, grabbed another can from the cooler to temper his dismay at the fall of civilization, squeezed it dry. Burped. "What happen, you flip him off?"

"Had to. Really didn't want to make his clients feel funny, but he was burning me. Cutting in line, shit, you learn not to do that in kindergarten. Gotta retrain these gunsels somehow."

"Too true. Did he yell at you?"

Skip laughed. "No. The clueless snot log flipped *me* off, like somehow I shouldn't take offense at his complete lack of flats etiquette. Talk about lowly evolved."

Kirby emitted a yeasty chuckle.

"That night I tracked him down, called him at home."

"No way, right?"

"Wrong. Had to. Guy thinks he can breathe my air like that, I couldn't rest 'til I squared it."

"What'd he say?"

Skip smiled at the memory. "Turned out more like what *I* didn't *need* to say. Shelly told me afterward that she knew by the lo-ong silences on my end of the line—just where and for how long—every time the fly speck rolled over and exposed his throat."

"I love a happy ending."

"Yeah."

Kirby wheezed out a laugh, said, "Catch this. Guess who got seen fishing under the bridge right next to Swabbie's, casting into them tarpon."

"Those things are handfed pets!" Skip shook his head. Tourists often visited this rustic landmark marina to witness, at hand's length, tarpon bigger than themselves. They could buy bags of fish guts, sorry, baitfish, and lob morsels directly into giant silver faces, take wet pictures. Quite a kick. The tarpon, although free to go wherever they wanted, recognized a free lunch when they ate it, and hung around close to the docks. "That's real sporty."

"It gets better. He was fishing a tournament. Said he was under the bridge to stay out of the rain."

"Right." Skip regarded tournaments as the antithesis of fly-fishing. In fact, he had come to have qualms about fishing tournaments in general, noticing how they often exposed some of the nastier traits of human character. Sure, folks could hang out and yak about how many and how big, like that mattered, but no law against shallow mindedness. The real negativity developed when a few players coveted victory so badly that they bent rules in their own hands. He lamented any erosion of honor among fly anglers. Hated to see secretiveness and dishonesty take root. Okay, some people got their rocks off on fishing contests, and if they craved those kinds of strokes, well, who died and made him god? A few of his buds fished them, won trophies. Still, he fiercely believed the heart of fly-fishing remained the game between angler and fish, the camaraderie with other fly fishermen. The clarity of focus gained from zeroing in on the natural world provided its own reward. If folks hankered after competition, why not shoot skeet? One of his favored clients put it best, "Fish a tournament? Like I really need to introduce some stress into my relaxation."

He looked to the west. Looked for direction, or point of beginning. Conch pink rays spilled across pale gold. The green hedge of mangrove shoreline had deepened, and blue had darkened and sifted through the sunset. He didn't want to run back to his dock at night. He didn't really want to give up hope on the worm hatch, either. Graphic hookups, explicit jumps, obligatory reel zings. Full frontal buzz, from when to where. "Gotta go on in," he conceded.

"That's cool."

"Yeah." Skip tasted a special moment, like amalgam-filled molars chomping aluminum foil. While his brain howled with resistance he steeled himself—for whatever karmic gymnastics or power surges it would take to end this slump, by god tomorrow. Somehow, some way, he would energize, *impel* his angler to hook up, to land, to *touch* a tarpon.

EIGHTEEN

 *Wishbone*

Guess the relentless Florida Keys sun has finally sucked this guide's brain dry. As his skiff idled homeward to their neighborhood boat ramp, Skip at first thought the figure on the dock might be some local guy curious if the bonefish had chewed today. But he kept getting smaller the closer Skip approached.

His wife Shelly claimed that some folks seemed to have a bigger aura than their actual physical stuff warranted, and Skip agreed he had seen a few of those "human beans." He'd seen that other category of smallness, too—people who diminish upon approach because they consist of innately vacant material. Lurking beneath a veneer as hollow as political promises, upon closer scrutiny they wither and cave in like a commissioner offered kickbacks. Skip now saw that the slight figure was actually a kid. A couple ragamuffin counterparts popped into view from behind the mangroves, raced across the grassy picnic area, took to their bicycles and shouted a volley of kid noises, hard to tell whether greeting or farewell.

"Hey," Skip said to the remaining kid, when his skiff thumped the dock. He walked beyond to his old pickup and backed it down the boat ramp. Set the emergency brake, *and* put it in gear. He'd found a guy he knew slumped beside the ramp one morning, still dark, regarding his boat, trailer, and truck, all totally submerged, with that ruined look of the suddenly bankrupt.

He rolled his shoulders, *Day's end feels damn good*. Poling clients around after bonefish may not equal plowing the back forty with a mule team, but it seemed like plenty of work to him. *After the boat gets washed I know the fridge will have a beer with my name on it. I don't want to keep it waiting*. He felt crusty with salt, anxious to hit the shower and scrub away layers of sweat that probably by now smelled like a steaming pile of beauty.

"You a guide?"

The boy drifted nearer while Skip winched the boat onto the trailer. The summer sun had burned brown from the kid's hair and spread it on his face and bony arms. Banged up knees and shins, outdoorsy sort. Looked about ten, twelve, though Skip didn't consider himself a good judge of age. Hell, most the time he still felt pretty damn young himself, despite those new gray strands he glimpsed in the mirror.

"Yeah."

"Cool."

Skip grinned at the kid and shrugged, "It depends." He knew that when his clients landed a bonefish, or jumped a man-sized tarpon, their happiness would flood into his own, doubling the take. On balance came the surge of regret when one snatched the fly away from an onrushing tarpon, missing the shot. Then he'd hear, "But I didn't *see* that fish," making him wonder, *What was this guy looking at, if not his fly?* He often got a kick out of those minutes spent redlining it, skimming over the water, eating the perception of speed like ice cream. Other times the drone of the outboard would shape a cocoon of privacy—moments that could provoke a deep contentment. He would notice that whatever stunning hue the wind and sunlight had created with the sea today, turquoise? peacock? well, it sure beat hell out of staring at the putty-colored walls of an office. Some days the water would take on the sheen of a teal's wing patch. *Now there's a piece of art.*

"I'd like to be a guide someday," the boy volunteered. He stared up at Skip as if to absorb some essential guide-like quality from the visual contact. He rubbed one bare foot against his shin; it had a large white scar near the small toe, looked something like a wishbone. *Funny, Shelly has one right about there, too, almost that same shape.*

"Hard work. Your folks probably have better plans for you," Skip replied, stepping into the cab of the truck. "Gotta go, see you later."

The kid nodded and trotted toward his bike, leaning against a palm tree in the neighborhood park.

Skip considered what the boy said, and wondered what kind of storybook mumbo-jumbo made the life of a fishing guide appear so goddam glamorous to an outsider. You might spend your day with a client so sun stunned that he'd muster just enough liveliness to fog a mirror, while you agonized the whole time, "How in the hell can I get this powder puff a fish?" He thought about how he always shifted into overdrive, poled faster, harder, struggling to *force* something to happen whenever the bonefish played hide and seek. How his eyes needed to spot fish so far away that he'd bump into next week. And all this for a guy so flats blind that he could have a bonefish in the boat before he ever saw it. Days like that had a sense of duration akin to a geologic age.

Of course, some of his anglers possessed such a radical sense of humor that it even helped assuage the pangs of fishlessness. Somewhat. Like LOO-ZAR THE MAGNIFICENT. *Yes,* this droll client would declare, this self-proclaimed comic book hero—*I am known as Loo-zar, able to fly to Florida in a single day, able to manage a business and beget heirs—but not, oh no, able to catch a bonefish.* They would laugh till their guts hurt.

As the fall bonefishing charters kept trickling in, Skip noticed the kid hanging around the docks a few times, fishing with a couple pals. Often the boys shared a rod between them, dangling some mystery bait into the emerald deep of the canal. Though small tarpon arched and rolled nearby, Skip doubted the boys ever caught much but a few snapper that schooled around the crusty pilings. They would clamor for news of his fishing day and he would brief them on the highlights and lowlights before heading home.

He described those days when not a single ripple bent the water—calm, flat, slick. The bonefish would tear a little hole in the surface film, you could almost hear it rip, the only sound around. It looked like skin then, the water. Permit, he told them, were the fish best at it, they seemed to slice through the water with their scalpel fins. Sometimes you would get the impression that permit could unzip the water and poke out their fins, just long enough to tantalize, then zip it back up without ever causing a disturbance. Not a dimple anywhere near where you saw them.

He told of certain days when it appeared that his chosen flats had drawn a crowd, and his attention would need to momentarily shift. As some unknown proto-guide, likely still on training wheels, attempted to encroach, Skip would dance with intimidation. Shoving after fish all the while, directing his angler to cast, strip, glancing up, blocking Proto's path, backing him down. He enjoyed teaching The Dance: poling, aiming, that fury of influence, that sheer force of will. Sweat and anger. Guiding as a contact sport.

The annual Kid's Day rolled around, a free-of-charge fishing clinic for any youngster able to finagle a way to attend. A good many members of the local guides association felt it important to their community to help out, teach area youngsters a few of the skills. Their lives hinged on fishing, so it only seemed natural to further the knowledge.

Skip showed up with a mental wheelbarrow full of calm and patience, ready to demonstrate casting to a mob of rambunctious and excited youngsters. He hoped he could help a few of the shy ones summon up the fortitude to enter the casting match after lunch. Although match seemed too strong a word for it, since every child who took part received a gift anyway, donated by Keys businesses. Still, it added a sense of accomplishment to those who improved enough to place in the standings. Their names would appear in the local paper, too, pretty heady stuff to a kid. Skip simply liked witnessing that glow spread across proud little faces.

"Hey," the kid said, popping out of nowhere while Skip strung up a fly rod. The wishbone scar on his foot sported an athletic shoe, but the earnest face still wore summer freckles. "Capt. Myers said you're my teacher."

A stick-on paper name tag said, Hi, I'm Will. Skip said, "Howzit, Will. You still wanting to be a guide?"

"Well, I really *wish* I could."

He looked a little less confident, though, and Skip thought that might be okay. Encouraging a starry-eyed kid into such a difficult line of work may well send that kid off on the wrong tack. Sure, someone has to push a boat around, he supposed, take folks fishing, but every so often he would realize that he held no positive fix on just why he kept on guiding, himself. *Lack of prospects with comparable income, odds-on,* would quip his interior voice. Nonetheless, a couple of the thornier aspects of The Life these days *were* a little hard to bend his mind around. One, most civilians scored a guide's ability on his angler's performance, regardless if that particular client could fish better than he could knit. And two, even if you nailed a Grand Slam yesterday, that triumph wouldn't subtract one whiff from the stink of a skunk today. Every charter started from absolute zero, and the pressure to somehow sway your client, by hook or by magic, so that he knocks the ball out of the park, achieves his best fishing day ever, could crush you like a thousand atmospheres.

"You already know how to catch fish, right?"

Will nodded yes. He glanced sideways at the fly rod. "Not with that, though."

"Well, we'll teach you some basic fly casting. Lots of people these days want to fly-fish on the flats. If you go into guiding you'll need to be able to make any cast that you ask your clients to make." Will looked so worried that Skip hastened to add, "We don't expect you to do that today." And then, with a laugh, "But there will be a test!"

They traded the usual chitchat while practicing, and Skip learned the family had only moved to the Keys the prior year. "We saw a couple of Key deer, when we went all the way down to the end of the road," Will announced. "They really are small! One was eating grass right along the highway, with little forked horns covered with velvet. He watched cars go by and didn't even run away."

"Yeah, they are pretty blasé," Skip agreed. "Shelly and I saw a doe in downtown Big Pine Key one afternoon. Of

course, you know downtown, there's only that single traffic light. This miniature doe, a hair taller than a Labrador
retriever but pounds lighter, tiptoed up to the signal like
she wanted to cross at the intersection. We all slowed to a
crawl, stopped, while she scampered to her new favorite
side of the road."

Skip told Will how these innocent-looking Key deer
would often swim over to an exclusive resort on a neigh-
boring key. There, they nibbled and noshed through the
carefully tended and expensive landscaping—they doted
on hibiscus bushes—and the management dared not
even shoo them away, because of their protected status.
"Shelly swears they understand they can get away with
anything."

Shelly soon materialized, having pedaled over to the
park on her bicycle to join Skip for the lunch break. She
rummaged inside her backpack for their groceries, and
then, settling into plastic chairs, she and Skip watched the
horde of famished youngsters scarfing up donated sandwiches from a local delicatessen. "Quite a crowd;" she
spooned blobs from her cup of yogurt.

In between bites of ham on rye, Skip explained that the
kid who wanted to be a guide had shown up to learn fly
casting.

"Honest, Shell, I don't know if I ought to encourage him
with this fantasy or not. Probably his folks would just as
soon he went to business school, or some other suit future.
That's the one, there."

"Oh, I've seen him, he and his kid sister helped pick up
branches in our yard from that last little tropical storm, in
October. You had to take the motor in for service that morning, remember? Anyway, fishing is a lot healthier than some
things kids get into, anymore. Knowing how *you* love the
outdoors, I'd bet you're not the only one who'd go crazy in-

side four walls." Life with Skip had long since made her aware that certain individuals chose their occupation more with an eye to the challenge than for what it paid. A job that defined their take on life, in some fundamental way.

Skip laughed and conceded that riding herd on papers from an office chair couldn't rival the exhilaration of screaming hell-bent over a limitless sea. But that desk guy wouldn't get hammered by ultraviolet light, either, or choused around by dangerous squalls. He reminded her of the morning a Bolt From the Blue had struck a mere arm's length behind his boat, and pointed out that several of their friends had begun having slices of their noses and ears peeled off at the doctor's office. If the lightning doesn't catch you, the skin rot will.

"Capt. Sunshine," she chuckled and shook her head. She prompted him, "Still, you have more days off than someone who works nine to five—well, not counting tarpon season."

"Yeah, days off with no pay."

When the session resumed, she lingered long enough to hear Skip explain some of what he considered the facts of fishing to Will.

"You'll have to remember now, if you decide to get into this game, you won't want the other guides to call you a One-spot Wonder. You'll need to discover your own fishing spots, for every stage of the tide. And when you start hunting for those spots, you'll notice right away that the fish aren't spread evenly throughout the waters, like the peanut butter is on your bread. Rather, they seem to congregate in lumps. Think of it more like eating a frankfurter on sandwich bread instead of a bun—a lot of the main course is all bunched up in one place and you find nothing but plain bread in the rest."

Will nodded solemnly, soaking up the nuggets of fishing lore. He had concentrated on his fly casting technique with that unsullied focus that Skip had noted in many young- sters learning to fish. Women picked it up rather easily, too, since most of them lacked the preconceived notion that they already knew everything about the subject. Grown men, though, often carried considerable hormonal baggage. Some had a tough time admitting to another male animal that they—just possibly—might not possess bound- less expertise in the business at hand. A few wouldn't lis- ten at all, and would repeat the same bungles all day, with mechanical precision. Like trying to cast their spinning rods with one hand. They had seen someone do it once on television, Skip supposed. Of course, they didn't possess the same proficiency as Mr. TV, so their control suffered. Casts would end up, *well, you don't want to know where*. He'd begun to think of this quirk as one of those koans: *What's the sound of one hand casting? Dammit!* Anyway, that pesky ego stuff could really shoulder itself into the way. Shelly'd say, "macho posturing" and, should he un- wittingly stumble into its grip, never hemmed and hawed about the impression such conduct gave: Absurd.

While Will doggedly stuck with his casting, Skip delib- erated more over the guide bidness. He mulled over those days when the sun pressed down so hard, its weight felt hot enough to blanch the blue from your eyes. Other times when, because of gusty winds, his anglers couldn't manage even routine shots at schools of approaching tarpon. *Slate torpedoes, incoming!* His clients would start babbling and stressing, tense and sucking it up so hard that Skip would bet their sphincters made a perfect vacuum—hell, if not for their shorts and underwear, their fly lines would prob- ably disappear up their butts. So Skip would shag the fish, working the meandering strings with his skiff, driving it forward, drifting back, fighting the force of the wind to maneuver the perfect angle. Next morning he'd be stiffer than a wedding dick, definitely stiffer than the prior day's wind, every tendon strained into raw protest. *Okay, every now and then he* didn't *feel all* that *young.*

On the matter of tarpon, he puzzled over how some anglers would fall apart like a cheap watch and get handcuffed—by dithering, wavering so long that they let the tarpon swim up too close, so near to the skiff that they couldn't make a cast. Because if the situation required a fast shot at twenty feet, "Quick, just roll it out there, now!" well, plenty of clients had the big boomer casts down pat, those 80-footers, but completely lacked a short game. Or perhaps these guys had only succumbed to another aspect of The Tarpon Effect. Clients sick with this malady would begin to flinch, missing the cast or the hookup (subconsciously) on purpose, out of (subconscious) fear that they might have to endure another muscle-wrenching bout with a powerful tarpon. They had come to realize that these fish break stuff for a living—fly lines, fly rods, noses if you ducked too close to remove the hook. Happened to some guide every tarpon season. So, you not only had to put these guys on fish, you needed to outmaneuver their psyches so they wouldn't roadblock their own way to success.

He remembered a bull session with a fellow guide during a previous tarpon season. After several minutes of gnashing their teeth, bitching about the fickle behavior of the tarpon that day, talk had turned to the delicate touch sometimes required to handle weak anglers. This guide had grumbled, "Maybe I *was* a little hard on the guy, but I'd rather he didn't go home and say, 'Yeah, my guide was a helluva nice guy, but I didn't catch a fish.' I'd rather he said, 'Well, he tuned on me quite a bit but I caught the biggest tarpon of my life.'"

Skip watched Will's timing, then told him to shorten up his forward stroke a bit, add more snap. He added, "Soon as you've mastered this first part of casting, you can begin thinking about the second part. Working on the fish's head. Getting the fly to the fish, that's a given, or should be, but then comes your retrieve, and the most vital part: knowing how to *make* the fish eat."

Will looked momentarily bewildered—what he had begun to think a doable task had just grown branches into the infinite. Then he resumed.

Skip grinned, went back to his observations. Aw hell, who knew? Pointless to worry about whether he might accidentally influence this kid to squander his life—it was his to squander. Besides, maybe in twenty years Will would develop into one of the premier guides. People start quoting his remarks.

He recalled how hard he and Shelly had laughed last tarpon season. He had gleefully related the terminology coming out of the mouths of some newbie guides, the ink still wet on their captain's licenses—Gits, his buddy called them, Guides-in-Training. "Meaningful Follow." They had liked that one a lot, and mused, could this mean when these neophytes think a tarpon *intended* to bite? If so, then how would a tarpon act during a "Meaningless Follow?" "An Eat." What these novices called that wink of time when the tarpon opened its mouth, as if trying for the fly, even though it missed. Hey, what if the fish had only grown bored by an angler's retrieve, or indifferent to yet another wrong color fly, and so what this tarpon had really done was—yawn? "A Bite." Okay, there you go with a traditional term, that eternal instant when the tarpon actually chomped down on the fly. Anglers of mortal insensitivity, having failed to discern this tick soon enough to react, and keen to cover this lack by denial, need only check their sandpapered leaders to verify the humbling truth. However some of the tyros who dredged the deeper waters, those given to flights of hyperbole, would tell their anglers that any bump from a ladyfish or a pinfish or a goddam trunkfish, was actually "A (tarpon) Bite." No guys, sorry, that's A Reach.

Everyone also recognized the well-established "Jump" —that exhilarating moment when your angler hooked up to the tarpon long enough to cause it to explode, bursting into the air in a fit of dismay. No mistaking this one. Nonetheless, some rookies couldn't stick to reality if they had contact cement for brains. Skip had dearly loved it when one of them told him how many "Bites" and "Jumps" his angler had attained on a given day, and came up with an incredible number. Like fifteen, when everyone else in the Keys felt damn lucky to air one or two because the fish just weren't chewing all that well. Skip had cackled and said, "Damn, Shell, swear I'm gonna book this guy, learn how a real pro does it!" This Rookie obviously not knowing that Skip and his client had fished a quarter-mile behind his boat all afternoon. They clearly saw that from *Rookie's* boat, not a single tarpon raged into the sky. Nice try, kid. The time-honored "Whiff" had long proved a valuable term, referring to when your angler stolidly obstructs the tarpon's every effort to "Eat," or "Bite," by missing the hookset. And finally, they had decided to throw in the one that Shelly—adopting the giddy mood of all this coinage— had described as "A Visual." As in "Visual Slam," wherein you only needed to *spot* the target species.

"I can't always make the fly land where I want it to." Will wrinkled his brow and looked out over the patch of lawn and the plastic hoop he had thrown at for the last several minutes.

"We've got quite a little breeze today, so you're doing good. Very good, in fact. You cast better than a lot of my clients already," Skip laughed quietly.

When the casting trials rolled around, Will placed first in his age group. Skip thought he had never seen a happier kid, and he felt pretty damn good about it, too. While the reporter from one of the local weeklies snapped shots of a beaming Will, Skip packed up his gear, still pondering The Life. Trying to make sense of it all. He recalled that day last spring when he and his client had encountered an Attack Tarpon.

On that muggy, calm, gloomy afternoon, the sky like a sheet of tin, he stood on the casting deck with his angler. A cloudburst had chased them to cover earlier, and now distant thunder echoed across the backcountry. To Skip's nose, the rain-fresh air carried the scent of moving tarpon. Having staked the skiff at a likely place along one of the well-known Tarpon Trails, he began the struggle anew. With a miracle, he would get this edgy angler hooked up. Tension poured from his tightly wrapped client, *No safer vault than a tarpon angler's asshole,* Skip decided. In order to properly align the boat, this site required both his pushpole jammed into the sand at the stern, as well as a very short, stubby stakeout pole to secure the bow.

His angler, Knowbetter, had fiddled all day changing flies—he kept tying on new patterns every ten minutes like he was fishing a goddam trout stream, even though Skip remarked, "They're not eating that color right now." *This guy is so nervous he probably wears his clothes out from the inside.* He jiggled his fly line, anxious, twitching it here, there, swooping it into cowboy loops.

"Quit throwing your line around," Skip warned him, "You won't be ready when the fish comes."

Sure enough. While Knowbetter squirmed and wiggled, a great tarpon swam directly down upon them. It slipped through the salt, brazen and polished, appearing to stir not a single fin. Swam, bang into their path, right to the stakeout pole, attached mere inches below the bow, inches from Skip's motionless and Knowbetter's happy, wriggling feet. At once its great eyes rolled in surprise: Boat! Pole! Humans!

The Attack Tarpon detonated, blew up like a metallic volcano, organic, charged with nitroglycerine. Mercuric jaw level with these interlopers, it stared them down with a dangerous glare, cratered the water scant inches before them, drenched them with habitat.

"One more attack like that one and we won't be coming out here any more!" Skip had spluttered to his angler. That jolt had engraved a vivid image on his brain.

Now, stowing the rod tube in his truck, waving goodbye to Will, he thought, Yeah, maybe life *didn't* get any better than that.

Honestly though, going nose to nose with the Attack Tarpon would have stoked him just as much, being the Angler, and letting some wishbone kid with a face like an affidavit play the Guide.

NINETEEN

Jet Skis for Jesus

"Jesus, Skip, maybe you just ought to hand me a hollow point," groaned Skip's angler, Willy (not his real name). Referring to a fly. The tarpon had roundly snubbed Willy's efforts so far today and his humor had begun to reveal a tinge of wry desperation.

Morning sunshine penetrated the waters of Florida Bay—forget about where—and ignited sparks on verdigris tarpon backs. They glistened, iridescent, looking flecked with pyrite along their spines. Their fins glowed pink as the flesh of salmon, an image mismatched to this subtropical radiance, so far removed from icy streams. Several dozed near the surface, a few looped into a daisy chain now and then, others free jumped like frisky kids on trampolines. Skip preferred to think that the majestic creatures leaped from sheer elation, an excess of spirit, rather than any fusty scientific reason. You could smell them strong today, their fresh green musk of mother ocean. He would bet not one of these happy tarpon gave a husky copulation about Willy's itch for Fulfillment.

"Is it time yet?" Willy grinned now.

He wanted to know if his scheduled Whine Time had arrived. "You have one minute to whine, on the hour," Skip had needled him a few years back. Right after relating a story about one of his guide friends. At the end of a long, tough fishing day, this guide had advised his irritable clients: "Next time just bring the cheese, ya got enough whine already." He sure had a way with words.

Skip chuckled, "Twenty minutes." Knowing he could probably get Willy casting to fish, or tell him a joke and he would forget about it for another hour.

Willy coiled the leader of his Apte Too, said, "Okay, how about that secret fly?"

Skip handed him a certain bunny fly, thinking, *Well, it's kinda secret. Just me and a couple other buds use this style collar. So far. Guess you could consider it a hollow point—it makes good tarpon food.* He knew he would prefer to use a harsher tool for the true antagonists around here.

Jet skiers. Just like one spoiled potato will damn sure rot the rest in the bag—and god, you ever smell one?—so the minority of angelic beings who amused themselves harmlessly astride those aquatic motorcycles became tainted. By association they gathered the same bad vibes as those numerous others who could give lessons in buttheadedness. But then everyone knows life sucks.

"Willy, try to remember on your next shot, throw at the *front* of the *mouth* of your fish, when it's aiming right at you. A straight down the fairway shot. Head On."

For some reason his clients couldn't understand that they needed to cast at the FACE of their fish, in FRONT of the fish and in a LINE with its path, rather than leading it as if they were swinging a shotgun on ducks. Skip had about halfway decided to draw a diagram and keep it on the boat, show them how the angles should look. A crossing shot, say a ninety-degree angle, has a very low rate of success. The tarpon probably wondered why this dumb foodstuff would travel toward them instead of scurrying away to safety, and rightfully so. Generally—if you dared venture that far with predicting fish behavior—those tarpon who adhered to the "you are what you eat" theory, at least, firmly declined to partake of stupid food. Blew him away. Not only how savvy the tarpon could act, but that he would expend mega-sweat to line the boat up just so, trying to give his anglers a clean head-on shot and then, swear to god, most of them would wait until the fish had moved to a crossing shot before they threw the fly.

"Gotcha."

Of course, then a day like that one last week comes around. Skip's poor befuddled twenty-foot fly-slingers had persisted with bumbling their chances by throwing crossing shots at every single school of tarpon. Exclusively. *Hell, at least they managed to get their casts in the Atlantic. And damn it all if a tarpon didn't just wheel, well, fin right out of its track, make a hard turn, and flare its pecs.* Stopping, it waited for the drifting fly to clear its eyes, reach its mouth—then it elevatored up, opened, turned, then YES! HOOVERED IT!

And to Double Your Hell, another fish ate the fly twice. So when it comes to tarpon you never know and Skip figured he might as well shut up. That lucky moment dissolved into its nasty opposite, though, when Skip noticed the fly line (his, not the client's) caught under the stripping guide. He cringed as the plastic coating peeled like an apple—the moment stretched by futility to a strobe of slow motion. While the tarpon scraped line against metal with her assault on the sky, he saw his earnings well pared by replacement dollars. At least the line broke instead of his fly rod.

"Willy, you see that fatty?"

A tarpon shaped like a tuna, six feet of chubby football, free jumped, a very long cast away. Kersploosh!

"Wow!"

Skip checked the brim on Willy's cap. Okay. He valued a mile-long brim on a client hat, it helps a guide tell where they're REALLY looking. "Yeah, I see 'em," they say, and half the time your guy's looking one-eighty away from the fish, particularly in the case of evanescent bonefish. Conjuring "vision fish" superimposed by the client's eager mind onto empty water. Now if they could only put a nice dark stripe down the center of the brim, to go with the Mickey Mouse watch hands he had threatened to paint on the casting deck.

Another singular day in what local folks call the backcountry. An occasional airplane moaned toward Miami miles overhead, a distant skiff would growl to a new spot, but otherwise the silence thundered, a pulse in your ears. Low leafy islets dotted the panorama, some festooned with such bird life they grew pungent with guano. Expanses of glassine brine mirrored vast delft sky. Aquamarine and pea soup green wavered and shifted places, the shades fleeting under towers of whipped cloud potatoes. An ambience of freedom.

Personally, though, Skip had resented fishing the backcountry ever since the Feds had decided to shake down guides. Take a handful of working stiffs who cared deeply for this ecosystem—a requisite or they would destroy their own livelihoods. Suddenly announce that they must begin paying to run their skiffs across waters of a park they already support with taxes. Willy had commiserated, saying,

"That doesn't sound fair," when they discussed the extortion. *No shit.*

At any rate, other citizens didn't have to fork over an extra tax to run their boats in the back, so guides had felt a trifle singled out. And oh yeah, the paperwork. Couldn't just bust their butts to put their clients on fish anymore, oh no-oo-oo, gotta fill out detailed reports for every day, every species, every size, blah blah blah. Paperwork reduction act—right. Okay, the catch reports might help the fish biologists monitor the resource, but since when did they need to know how much money the guys earned while fishing backcountry waters?

Willy had gasped when he heard that. "They want you to what?"

And not like they ever preempted any valuable ranger time; they rarely saw them. The rangers all hung out at Flamingo answering tourist questions. *Oh, well, excuse me*, Skip amended his thoughts. *I saw a ranger a few months back. No, wait, that was a state park guy, not even back here.* While bonefishing he had happened across a blue heron caught in monofilament, thrashing around in the shallows. Poor sucker couldn't move, so Skip called park headquarters on his VHF. A bird that size can put your eye out with its beak, so he dared not let his clients help. The stater held its wings, Skip wrapped a boat towel around the pointy end, and they proceeded to untangle one honking, blatting, pissed off heron. Skip didn't even snitch a feather off him, but he did cuss the sumbitch irresponsible enough to trash their water. Not like proper line disposal's a big damn secret.

Today, however, in calendar terms, had reached a Weekend. Fishing on the ocean side would likely expose Willy (not his real name) to aggravations from frothy-lipped Miami jet skiers, invading the Keys to avoid their more tightly regulated waters at home. Hell, they couldn't scream around in Biscayne National Park anymore, so guess where they would all go now? And for some reason, today Skip simply hadn't felt like yelling his lungs out.

Certain days he woke up primed, fired up with the right frame of mind to rant at any menacing jet skier that dared trespass. Wave runner, whatever. *Why, then, don't they ride their macho asses out past the reef on the real waves,* he thought. Instead they zip across shallow waters terrorizing the bonefish, spewing racket, fumes, and mayhem. And zoom dangerously close to flats boats, splashing anglers who want to catch those fish. Of course, a fish with the size and dignity of a tarpon won't necessarily spook and split for Brazil, like an edgy bonefish. Instead, they merely tend to sink lower in the water and refuse to bite, or to rev up their pace a notch and glide resolutely onward in search of calmer seas.

Which seemed like a good idea now, since this tarpon action had slowed. They were rolling a little still, but moving on as they did so. "Hey, we're gonna make a run," Skip told Willy, as he poled away from the fish, "not far, you won't need to rack your rod."

Speaking of rod racks, Skip had damn near decided he needed brain racks instead of rod racks on his skiff. Maybe nice cool roomy kegs of beer, so his anglers could park their brains and keep them in high spirits, and then maybe they would listen to what their guide told them instead of thinking wrong. Moving the fly when he said stop, stopping the fly when he said slow it down, jerking it out of fish lips when he said leave it. *Yeah, beer kegs.*

Willy parked himself on the cooler, holding his fly rod. He lit a cigar. Before Skip cranked the outboard he noticed that Willy had let his fly line drool behind the boat, *Going to get in the prop.*

"You're in the motor," he cautioned.

Willy stuffed the cigar between his teeth, pushed his rod forward and tried to get hold of the line—that action promptly wrapped the slack fly line around Skip's neck. Thick gray ashes dribbled across the deck. "Rolling on the floor, laughing my ass off," Skip sputtered, trying to extricate himself from the web. One of his favorite clients, Willy.

During the brief putt to another basin, Skip noticed no other vessels nearby to spoil the quiet. No other guide boats—*hmmm*, maybe this spot had gone dry—no, more likely just out of favor this week. Funny, how guides would go through hot spot fads and forget all about these old boring places for a spell. At least no "personal watercraft" marred the scene. Long banned from Everglades National Park, they nevertheless violated these waters at will, because the rangers rarely patrolled the areas in their charge. In light of the backcountry ban, he often wondered why jet skiers were still allowed to render havoc on the ocean side flats, seeing as how the waters surrounding the Keys had now attained status as a marine sanctuary. He and his friends decided that they must simply be too slow on the uptake to figure out the hidden benefits of *that* worthy policy.

"Okay Willy, there they blow, lock and load." Skip let the boat coast to a stop quietly, unracked his pushpole, and began shoving them toward the bulging wakes of meandering tarpon. In the echoing silence you could hear the big creatures huffing as they took oxygen from the surface. Bloop, whooofff.

A couple big ones lay right in the surface film, so contented with their day that they glowed almost white, radiant and reflective. With every aspiration they rose slightly, broke the film, then settled back, just beneath. Tarpon nirvana.

And try to find a water cop when one of those nematodes scums you, Skip poled toward the blissed out fish and festered, worried about raucous interruption and overfull of acute jet ski remembrance. *They come scorching across a flat that you've just poled thirty minutes to access, one that was clearly marked with orange buoys: Closed to the Use of Combustible Engines. But guess where most of the water cops spend their quality time? Out at the reef, where the jet skiers ought to roam, scoping the babes on the scuba and snorkel boats. Pseudo judges in a sham bikini event, pissin' all over themselves like excited dogs.*

Skip loved dogs, although he and Shelly were without benefit of one just now. He even found it somewhat funny how often humans would simulate what dogs do in cars: screaming around in fast boats, or on jet skis for that matter, for apparently no good reason other than to feel the wind in their ears. But anyway, with all the law enforcers mired by the laws of nature, Skip often felt obliged to chastise miscreant jet skiers himself. Duty bound, even, to render a traditional boot camp tongue lashing. *You ignorant pukes! Etc.*

A half hour or so later, after he had grown weary from whiffing shots at tarpon, Willy opted for a lunch break. Massive thunderheads stacked up on the horizon, pressed against the wind and heat of the sun. Skip calculated their threat. He recalled the weather lies on the news this morning. You had to discount radically whatever chamber of commerce outcome they forecast, they of the slick helmet heads and mall hair. They apparently experienced their share of outdoor adventure between parking lot and studio, and, in the spiraling cultural trend that rendered appearance more important than content, would gleefully pronounce it a Nice Day Out There if you could see sunshine. Never mind that this "nice" goddam sun shines in the teeth of a gusty twenty-plus-knot wind that kicks waves over the bow of your skiff, trying to swamp it, and that the salt spray lashes your face while you struggle to pole, or cast. Yeah, loving every minute of those Nice Days.

Willy chomped into his onion roll, so Skip said, "Hey, let me cast your rod, see how it throws," and nabbed it while Willy chewed. And then he said, "Think I see something," and winged one out there and KABOOM! the tarpon felt metal—Skip pegged it on him.

Willy swore, spluttering mustard and ham, "You knew it! You saw it coming!"

Unraveling with merriment, Skip fairly cackled, "Hell, no, man, just a lucky shot—here, take this damn thing, I've gotta save my strength for pushing this boat around!"

Now this tarpon hookup hadn't possessed quite the same surprise factor (*yeah, saw a string of 'em cruising this way, thought it'd wake Willy's ass up to jump one in his face*) as this one day bonefishing, a while back. First thing in the morning they swooshed down at bonefish headquarters and Skip had started poling hard toward a wad of fish, his guy breaks out a bowl of cereal and milk. Swear to god. Bonefish tails sticking out of the water like your hair when you wake up and oblivious Brent crunches his oat flakes. And folks wonder why guides go nuts.

Willy struggled with his tarpon while Skip observed the cloud condos again, building up fast as Miami. Probably have to run for it later, dodge the usual afternoon thunderstorms. Lucky today, though. So far. Because Willy (not his real name) had achieved a certain fame, or notoriety, in the Keys for bringing Willy Weather with him whenever he dropped in for a fishing trip. Over the years they had fished and bitched and told lies together, didn't matter whether March or July, somehow Willy could manifest twenty-five to thirty knot winds or a tropical low pressure system with bucketfuls of falling water. Downright breezy fishing yesterday, cloudy the first morning, neither one quite the usual tarpon season weather, whatever that resembled. But decent today, therefore this year their Willy Days had been less than awful. So far. It worried the hell out of Skip. The day held time yet. Time enough for a water spout or some other Willy-caliber Weather to materialize.

A camera poked from the top of Willy's gear bag, so Skip pulled it out and snapped a shot of him sweating and swearing. Booosh! The tarpon exploded a section of water, transforming aqua to foam and he snapped again, hoping the camera caught that flash of sun on its silver jaw. This one kept jumping a lot, which makes a tarpon tire more quickly. A good thing, or Skip knew he would have to follow it with the boat. By the time the pooped fish came to the side of the skiff, ripe with its fresh green tarpon musk, and its huge armor-plated scales encasing all light, it had transmuted into Willy's Tarpon.

Skip had observed this phenomena before, whenever a guide hooked up and handed the rod over to a client, whether adult or child, man or woman. He reckoned it came, in part, from that intense single-mindedness an angler gave every twitch and nuance of the fish during their battle, and the fish's equally powerful drive to survive. Connected in opposition. And so it happened that two dissimilar creatures became familiar with each other's depth of will and strength. In any event the confrontation seemed to engender a link, and a proprietary air followed. Willy was a happy man.

Willy (not his real name) broke out a cigar to congratulate himself, asked where they planned to fish tomorrow. Even though the tarpon had been moving the ocean in good numbers, their choice of fishing location would depend primarily on what weather transpired, always chancy with Willy in town. But Skip explained to him, too, about the diciness of weekends and what to expect in case they ventured out front.

Willy laughed out loud. "Listening to a local radio station on the way to the boat ramp this morning, they were going on about some jet ski races somewhere this weekend, and the guy interviewing the leader of this jet ski group asks him, "Hey, what about this talk we hear of jet skiers harassing flats boats and all that," and the group leader goes, "Oh no, we don't do anything like that. We ride jet skis for Jesus.""

TWENTY

 *Tarpon: Wane to Wax*

"Hey, Captain, where's the fish?"

Skip's angler acted restless and grumpy. He showed no interest in the bronze sea turtle paddling by, or the pair of white ibis in flight. Skip pointed them out to lighten the mood, share the local wonders. But it seemed that this guy thought of a day on the flats as a desperate contest for status. *If he hooks up he'll damn sure get his contest. Now if he would help look for fish instead of carping.*

A thank-god school of tarpon loomed, dark as a thundercloud across the flat. "Here they come! Two hundred yards, twelve o'clock!"

"Where?"

His angler peered at the crystal blue water in front of his shoes, then jerked his head around to challenge Skip. Disbelief stained his face. He couldn't see the fish because his twelve o'clock began where his toes pointed, instead of the bow of the skiff. Still. Skip tried again.

"Point your rod! More right. Your other right! Good, there, see that big dark shape over the white sand patch?"

"Oh, yeah. So? Where's the tarpon from there?" His voice grated, abrupt and edged with demand.

"Those *are* the tarpon." Skip prayed he wasn't really flats blind.

"About time!"

The huge cloud of tarpon glided toward them. Their approach was silent, unlike the blood pounding in Skip's ears. A slight chop made irritating watery pats at the fiberglass hull; his angler's restless feet shuffled counterpoint, while his reeking sunscreen cloyed in the thick hotness of the morning. Gobbets of it clung to the side of his pallid cheeks and streaked the backs of his pink knees. It remained a mystery why he had waited to apply it on the boat. A man who would rather give directions than read them, rather ruin the gear and spook the fish.

"Okay now, untangle your fly line and get ready."

He looked down and saw himself standing on the fly line. He probably didn't recall that he had kicked at it, too. "Oh shit!" The line lay twisted into limp curlicues on the hot deck. Knot larvae. He grabbed at it, his movements angry, frantic, clumsy.

"Check your fly, make sure there's no weed on it."

Despite Skip's frequent warnings, he couldn't remember to hold his fly in his hand, at ready. Instead he let it dangle loose alongside the boat, a magnet for weeds.

"Oooh shit!" He yanked at the line and found it fastened underwater, maybe to a piece of sponge or turtle grass. It broke free and he set about removing the grass bass. His sneakers went bumpety bumpety as he fidgeted with the gear.

Time for a reminder that fish can hear. "You'll need to keep your feet still now. Don't want them to turn out."

But the dark vision kept coming, a shadow of quiet power as it drifted over the white sand. The tarpon floated without hurry, swimming high and happy, stopping to daisy chain now and then. Skip watched them from the tower, seeking a big one with a hungry attitude; they needed to find a dim bulb with kamikaze tendencies. Trickles of sweat stung down his back and the bottoms of his feet burned from standing. The tarpon had been slow to move today, making for a long tense hour since the last school came by. They had sensed no danger from Mr. Congeniality's haphazard casting, which he had hinted was somehow Skip's fault. A cruel thought, and it chewed at Skip's spirit.

"Don't let these get by me," his angler said like a threat. He started false casting now, too soon.

Although glad that he was standing ready, Skip feared he would burn out before the fish got here, and tried to calm him. "Just wait a minute, let them get closer. Then pick out your fish, don't flock shoot them."

"I know," he snapped, and stopped false casting for five seconds. Then he started up again like a wind-up toy out of control. "Got to get the feel of this outfit," he said, peevishness reddening his face.

"Helps to practice some before you get here." *A waste of breath.* They had discussed it on the phone, the need to go to a local fly shop and try out a larger fly rod. Considerable, the change from a five or six-weight rod to an eleven or twelve-weight; can throw off your timing until you get used to it. Bad moment to find that out, with the adrenaline juicing up your heart while the fish poured by at your feet.

He slapped the water with his backcast. "I know. I didn't have time."

"Okay, remember, lead your fish." *Not like the last bunch, one of which must have a ding in his snout from the fly.* But that cast *was* in the same zip code, unlike the first shot he had made. That one fell so far off line it was hard to believe that he had aimed for the same target. *Probably didn't.* With a sick dread Skip felt The Look bearing down on him from the near future. The Look that said your angler had forgotten all the shots at fish he screwed up, and blamed you for his defeat. All part of the agony of a fishless day with a surly client, and it gnawed a hole in him. Reality shined in. Skip's need to put Surly on fish, have him hook up, catch one, outstripped even Surly's need to be the hero.

"I know."

Skip glanced at the hot blue sky to see thunderheads piling in gray rumbles toward the Everglades. *Good—far enough away not to cast a white shadow on the water.*

Now the tarpon showed up as individuals, barely seeming to move in their spear-shaped flotilla, each one well over eighty pounds. A few big enough for a serious gear test stood out. The old rush of excitement pounded Skip's bones with an ache for a shot at these gorillas. Thoughts escaped: what about some townie job, have money for more than gear and boat upkeep; regular days off; hire some guy to put *him* on fish like these, stand on the *front* of the boat! Days like this did it. It made it double-tough to give his all when a guy came unprepared *and* oozed attitude. But no. No suit life for him—the flats were his office, he shall not gripe. "Okay, now start your cast."

Surly let one go. He deftly hooked himself in the back of one raw drumstick. The barbless hook dropped out with no problem, but meanwhile his talent with the fly line had sewn him into a bag. "Oooh shiiit!"

The lead fish slid by, quiet, indigo backs deeper now, as his angler unraveled the skein of fly line. Their big, smart eyes rolled up and looked at Skip's frustrated ones; their giant scales flashed with wet reflected sunlight. He wanted to tell Surly to hurry up and get another cast off, but this guy writhed with edginess already. It could take the whole day for some folks to calm down enough to listen, pay attention to what the fish do, figure out the gear. They got an expensive casting lesson, with real fish instead of hoops in a pond. But their lost chance at the magic of a jumping tarpon hurt deep.

"Take your time. There's a good string of them. They're close now."

"I know."

His angler started false casting again.

"You've got too much line out!" Skip warned him. "Shorten up on it!"

"Uuhhh!" Surly grunted as he cast the unaccustomed weight. Too far. The line furled out over the fish. A few of them saw it coming—some wrath from humanity sent to punish their salty innocence. They exploded into motion with the force of dynamite under water, a bulging hollow liquid echo. They reeled away from the stringy menace, leaving only boil and foam and their retreating bullet darkness.

"Oh shit! They're gone."

They damn sure were.

Failure. Lumps of gloom clogged Skip's heart. It was hard to swallow. This guy wouldn't have been happy if you hung him with a new rope. Now this.

"Let's go in. I've had enough," Surly grumbled.

"We've got a couple more hours," Skip pointed out. "Maybe you can hook up on the next school." He didn't want to cheat Surly out of any time, but he had to admit the idea held appeal. Tomorrow another new client arrived, and he could hope that this one had packed his eager attitude along with his sunscreen. At least he'd had the sense to book three days, enough to allow his expectations to adjust to his skill level.

The somber mood held fast while Skip sped the skiff into the wind, back to the dock, into tomorrow. *If the new guy can just hook up.* That was primary. A client may need the fight, may need to touch the fish, or take a picture. But for Skip, jumping the tarpon gave plenty. That moment when the fish believed and the angler realized it.

He hit his Reset button.

He stopped whining.

And he got up and went for it again. At first he didn't feel connected to himself; he reached for the light switch on the wrong wall, spilled the coffee. *Hung over with self-doubt.* He took an aspirin for the headache he knew he would probably have.

But his new angler's enthusiasm buoyed him, and when they reached the Tarpon Trail the fish made the first move, and the second. Skip's focus sharpened with each approach.

"There he is! Sixty feet! Point your rod!"

"I can't see him!"

Skip stood on the tower and cursed at the cloud that hid the sun, hiding the fish from his angler. He knew it was a personal insult. He knew it had gone out of its way to do this; no other clouds marked the burning sky. The shadow of the hateful cloud floated away at last, and now, instead of a silver mirror, the water turned translucent, a strange blue ochre. Heat clotted the air. Small mangrove covered keys shimmered in the distance, appearing to hover between water and sky. Smells of iodine, swamp muck, and watermelon nudged at the edge of his senses.

The big gray fin slipped up into view and broke the calm film of still-cool water in graceful silence. The giant tarpon floated near the warmer surface, its dark back positioned to absorb the heat of the sun. Things this beautiful made a short list.

Sweat boiled off Skip's face as he leaned his body against the pushpole, to turn the skiff to the best position for a cast. His tee shirt hung wet and limp as a washrag. The water was deep here. Hard poling. They couldn't get any closer or the fish would see them. He urged his angler on. Surely he could see the broad shiny back now. "Now! Forty-five feet! Don't line him! Ten feet further right! Right!"

"I've got him! Ohmigod!"

His suddenly pious angler had spotted the huge fish at last, and from the way his jaw dropped he must have been impressed. He was still waving his fly line in the air too much. *Probably so nervous that he's forgotten everything I've told him.* "Drop it! Drop it! Hurry! Now!"

Pious pulled himself together and flung his line toward the tarpon. Skip held his breath. Despite his claim of casting practice, he had blown his first two shots, horrifying the fish in the process. Pious was disappointed; Skip was more so. This one *had* to be good.

A finite number of shots like this occurred in any day; why did that come as a surprise to some people? Skip didn't know how they pictured it in their minds—an endless loop of shooting-gallery ducks? But fish were alive, with personalities and attitudes of their own. Only now and then did their wants coincide with our aims.

This time miracles happened—the cast landed where it should. Skip secretly thanked Pious for working on his double haul. "Good! Good! Now strip it! Faster! Good! Now slow it down! Strip it! Strip it!" He balanced on the tower, on a tightrope of helpful urgency and intimidation.

Trying to convey the necessary intensity through force of will and voice.

The tarpon slid through the clearness, huge shiny scaled body gliding with no visible effort. He acted lazy, bored, with no apparent concern for the small feathered hook he was moving toward.

Pious angler kept repeating, "Ohmigod, ohmigod!"

"Work it! Work it! *Make* him eat!"

Silvery pectorals flared, the tarpon kicked forward with a slash of his big forked tail. The metallic hinge of his jaw flashed, revealing a cavernous mouth. Hours went by in a burst of roaring silence; even Pious had quieted his desperate chant. The gorgeous fish slurped the fly like a gulp of lemonade on a hot day. Then he turned to swim away. He acted casual, unaware of the trap, going on about his tarpon business. Maybe thinking of the next morsel to be found, or a return to his sunbath.

"He ate it! Set the hook! Set the hook! Like you *mean* it!"

Time compressed, and expanded. Too much was going on but it took forever.

"Oh no! Ohmigod! What do I do?"

"Clear your line!"

His angler's sunburned knees shook. Skip hoped he kept his feet still and didn't stand on his line when it zinged out through the guides of his rod. If he would take off his shoes he could feel it when it got under his feet. Probably afraid of sunburned insteps. Pious jerked with his line hand, then again and again harder, when Skip yelled. Fly line swirled up from the casting deck in narrowing spirals toward him. His line arm flung out, out, out, tossing line in the air to untangle as it spun toward the rod. Skip remembered to breathe. "Don't move your feet! Bow! Bow! He's coming up!" He admonished, coached, warned.

"Ohmigod!" Pious grunted. He leaned forward in an awkward squat. Not pretty, but it worked.

The tarpon rose out of the water in what seemed like slow motion, bulging through the surface tension. The swirl grew and foam spun out, and it made a hollow sound like the vortex of a low-flying jet. A whoosh of warm fishy saltiness. He came up vertically, on his tail, as if a crane were lifting him. Going for a skyride. Cobalt and silver. A magic and prehistoric force twanging on the end of a space-age line.

Skip didn't know about Pious, but *his* heart thudded and bucked, knocking his ribs with big hard thumps. He loved this tarpon, his power, his outrage at being tricked. He didn't feel hot or tired anymore. He could pole for a hundred miles, further. In that moment, it was worth the long hours, the bad casters, the "days off" working on gear. This was why he did it. He cheered for his angler, for the awesome, beautiful fish, for himself. "All right! All right!"

About the Author

Sandy Rodgers has published stories and articles in *Gray's Sporting Journal, Fly Fish America, Saltwater Sportsman, Fly Fishing in Saltwaters, Sporting Classics, Saltwater Flyfishing, Trofeo Pesca, The Elements of Fly Fishing* and on the Website *Alloutdoors.com*. She has also been recruited to write for *Sportman's Adventures* television. Sandy and her husband, Bob, reside in the Florida Keys, where they collaborate as co-columnists for *Sporting Classics* and *Reel-Time.com*, and serve as Florida regional editors for *Fly Fish America*. Jaunts to destinations as varied as Mexico, the Ozarks, Iceland, and Honduras enhance their stockpile of images and lore as they continue living the dream.